THE TESTING

THE TESTING

A NOVEL

by

MELVIN BOLTON

LONDON
VICTOR GOLLANCZ LTD
1987

First published in Great Britain 1987
by Victor Gollancz Ltd,
14 Henrietta Street, London WC2E 8QJ

British Library Cataloguing in Publication Data
Bolton, Melvin
  The testing.
  I. Title
  823'.914[F]   PR6052.O4/

  ISBN 0–575–04058–0

Typeset at The Spartan Press Ltd,
Lymington, Hants and printed in Great Britain
by St Edmundsbury Press Ltd, Bury St Edmunds, Suffolk

THE TESTING

ONE

"THERE USED TO be a man who stood on Villiers Street during the morning rush from Charing Cross. He was incredible; he could play about six instruments at once."

"This chap's playing four, if you can call it playing."

"There's no pleasing you is there? Last time we came here we got a decent bit of Haydn and you complained it was dreary."

"I prefer these characters who do acrobatics. Now if those girls playing Haydn had all done handstands I'd have been fascinated."

"That is about your level," she said.

He winked at her. "Time for another one?"

"No, I really ought to be getting back, I'll be getting nasty looks again."

They stood up at the little outdoor table, gathering belongings. He shrugged into his overcoat because it was the easiest way to carry it. She put on sunglasses against the weak spring sunshine as they moved away towards Burleigh Street. At the Strand they stopped and he kissed her, "Be good."

"I'll try," she called above the din of the traffic.

He watched her walk briskly away then he turned and continued down the Strand towards Trafalgar Square.

He was still thinking about her when he crossed the end of St Martin's Place and entered the impressive stone edifice that is the Embassy of South Africa. He was late and, with his usual luck, he did not manage to slip in unnoticed. Still in his overcoat, and with a transient flush, he came face to face with Frits de Wet.

"Jesus! You wouldn't pass a breath test, Collins."

Christian Collins stood back. Behind the other's rimless lenses he could see no real danger signals. "I've only had a couple of beers, Frits. I met Sue for lunch at Covent Garden. That's the trouble with booze; two smells the same as ten."

"That's why they invented breathalysers. Who is on now?"

"Nick. I did a double stint this morning. Got up at quarter to dawn."

"You'll have to do a fill-in as well. Nick's being taken off at four."

"Okay."

"Right now do a check on our leads up top. I think they're clogged up again with pigeon crap." He squelched away on thick, synthetic soles. They were the only soft thing about him.

A predictable layer of pigeon guano had accumulated on the aerial equipment but there was nothing that could interfere with communications. He had explained that fact, more than once, but Frits de Wet was not a man you kept arguing with. If Frits wanted the antennae kept clean then it was easiest to clean them. He probably knew perfectly well that the birds had no effect on reception but they gave him a convenient excuse for keeping up an extra strict maintenance schedule. Collins scraped the cables and checked all connections. Diplomatic wireless technicians were supposed to look after the basic installation. His responsibility, strictly, was only for the additional equipment which the Department had installed, but as diplomatic and departmental business all went in and out through the same antennae he didn't worry about demarcation lines when he was on the roof.

For a time he leant on the ornate stone balustrade and gazed down into the square. The noises made by the bustling things below sounded impossibly loud. It was an acoustic effect which never failed to surprise him. He could recall visiting Trafalgar Square as a child. He remembered the fountains and the lion statues and his mother bending down to explain things to him. "See the springbok and the buffalo heads up there on that building? That's our *embassy*." Then she'd tried to tell him what an embassy was.

At ten to four he went down to the radio room. They called it 'records' and it was as good a name as any. It couldn't lead to confusion with archives because that was never known by any other name. Nick Pienaar was in headphones in front of a transceiver set and a small battery of tape recorders. He was also responsible for what looked like a miniature switchboard and a telex terminal. The functions of other items which cluttered a long

8

wooden table were more obscure, but one of them was clearly in the process of being repaired. Collins slipped on to a chair and began to fiddle with it. Pienaar swivelled round in his headset, moving his whole body as if he had a stiff neck. There was a book in his lap.

"Same problem, Chris. You can tell him this time. The old type was better, more reliable."

Collins nodded and continued to fiddle. Repairs and technical improvements were a relief from monotony and the only bit of challenge in the work. The routine was stifling.

At four o'clock Pienaar got up, stretched and yawned. "Over to you."

"How is it?"

"Quiet. A couple of class threes, nothing else."

Collins moved over, fitted on the headphones and adjusted the controls. It would be 5 p.m. in Pretoria, there was only an hour's difference during British summer time. Pienaar gave him a wave and went out. For most of the session Collins had nothing but his thoughts for company, for he had come without anything to read. At one point Jutta Keiner tramped in to collect her tapes. Only she was authorized to touch them and in Collins' time, at least, she had taken no leave and no illness. Collins wondered who de Wet would delegate if ever he found himself without Jutta. He watched her now, operating the combination lock which released a retaining bar over the numbered tapes. One by one she checked for the recording signal, then stopped the machine and replaced the reel. Conversation about them was taboo but the few who were authorized to enter 'records' knew full well what they were. They could only guess where the transmissions might be coming from but the same few names would have appeared at the top of everyone's list.

Cradling her box of tapes, Jutta retreated to her inner den. A widow of fifty-five, she was a grey lady from her hair to her skirt, and had she been a schoolteacher the little ones would probably not have liked her.

From a safe she collected a series of tapes with numbers marked in felt pen. Each contained recordings accumulated from a single source. The system was simple: at the end of a normal working day she would hear the latest 'takes' and then transfer them to the storage reels, erasing the originals so as to leave a clean tape to be put back in use. Sometimes, depending on sound quality or importance, she would set aside the original as well. Those of special interest might be duplicated and despatched to Pretoria by diplomatic pouch.

She would have welcomed a speedier system but there was no alternative to careful listening. Technically there was much scope for improvement but somebody still had to sit and hear the stuff through and decide what, if anything, might be useful. That had to be done no matter how sophisticated the equipment.

Experience and a phenomenal memory had made Mrs Keiner an expert. She could quickly sift through hours of listening in the way that other people scan the newspapers — picking out the headlines and items of interest without wasting time on the rest. There were no blank periods on her tapes because the recorders were only activated by the receipt of a transmitted signal.

It was a single word that caught her attention, a name, and the most common one in England at that. Yet she reacted instantly and her fingers jerked at the controls. "Contact again," she murmured, as she wound back for a repeat. The digits put the recording time at 14.45 and she noted this as she tuned for higher fidelity.

"Hello (pause). Yes I have. The arrangements for a sample are acceptable (pause). Hello? Mr Smith . . . ?"

Frowning now, and with a new alertness, she turned her attention to the storage tape, this time looking intently at the display panel and going very slowly. She stopped the reel and brought it carefully back to a 'take' that had been made five days previously.

". . . talk privately."

"We will not be disturbed here."

"I would prefer to talk outside. You know what they say, walls have ears."

"Not these walls I think. Please say your business."

"Well, let me say just this: I represent someone who has genuine sympathy with your cause. We believe we can help by supplying you with, er, an advantage that will be the most powerful single factor in your struggle. We believe it could entirely tip the balance for you (here there was a long pause). I am completely serious. Believe me, I'm not joking and I am not a crank. I'm certainly not drunk either."

"I can see that. But, you know, we have friends all over the world who are willing to help us. The trouble is that we are like David against an army of Goliaths. With the best sling in the world we have to flee the battlefield after every blow. So what sort of advantage can you be talking about? A political one perhaps?"

"I wouldn't waste your time. You've had world opinion on your side for decades and it's got you nowhere. No, I'm talking about something that none of your friends can offer you. An advantage that's exactly what David needs."

"Tell me more."

"Not here."

"Where do you want to go?"

"Anywhere in the open — you lead the way."

"And you insist that we are alone?"

"No, I must insist that we talk alone but I have no objections to others being nearby. Mr Tamala, if I had some other motive for wanting you outside I need only have waited for you to leave. I have come here instead of sidling up to you in the street because I decided to approach you openly and in a proper manner. You can take whatever precautions you like."

At this point there was another long pause and then:

"Very well, Mr Smith. Let us step outside."

An errant lock of springy hair dangled on the wrong side of Jutta's headband but she ignored it. With quick, practised movements she played the new 'take' once more and then returned to the earlier recording. "It has to be," she whispered to herself. And she allowed the tape to continue.

". . . step outside." There were noises of chairs moving after that and a door closing. The office was then quiet for nearly two hours if the time display was to be believed. After that period the recorder had been reactivated by Tamala returning and making a phone call:

"Tamala here. I have to talk to you (pause). Yes (pause). I know that, but this could be an emergency (pause). No, not that but it could be just as important (pause). That would be good; I will be there. Thank you."

Mrs Keiner passed a hand over her tired features and sat back, staring into space. She wondered how de Wet would react and how his reactions might affect the team. Whichever way she looked at it there appeared to be an awful lot of overtime ahead. She spent a few minutes in preparation and then went to see her chief just before he was due to leave the office.

He could tell before she spoke that she rated her news highly. "It's your crackpot," she announced. "He's not so crazy after all. They seem to think he has something. It's all ready for you," she added, before he could ask.

In her den it was de Wet's turn to sit silently at the machine, and all he had to do was listen. She had put the 'takes' in sequence for him — Smith's approach to Tamala; Tamala's subsequent request for an urgent meeting with a third party, and the latest news that Smith was being taken seriously to the extent that a sample of whatever he was offering was acceptable on his terms.

De Wet spun a finger to ask for a replay and when it was finished he dragged off the headphones and slapped the table with the flat of his hand. "We should have had a phone tap in there months ago!"

Jutta inclined her head but it was non-committal. Not her business. "It has to be as it sounds I think," was what she said.

"Of course it is. Whoever he is, Smith has got them interested. He must have *something* they like the sound of."

"And I suppose it has to be his big comrades that Tamala was calling."

"Who else? Who else would he run to when something too big for him to handle is dropped in his lap? The little fool was probably straight through to Kensington Palace Gardens. We might even have got his contact on tape if only we'd had a phone tap in place. Oh, it's what it seems all right. Keep on to it, Jutta. Bring the intervals down to an hour if you can and let me know immediately you get anything more." He shook his head. "I still find this hard to take seriously."

De Wet conferred with Danny Meester that night. Meester was, officially, his deputy but he had been in London for less than a year and had not, in his own opinion, been fully accepted in the role. On the other hand he had a measure of independence because he was responsible for several agents in Britain and he knew each of them far better than did de Wet. De Wet did not deny it but that night he was less than impressed by Meester's little network.

"We know nothing about him," he was saying. "Although if we'd put a phone tap in we might have known a bit more."

"Frits, we have been over this before. A phone tap is out of the question as long as we've got Nero there. He's a good agent, worth more than any number of phone taps."

"I hope so. Right now I'd gladly trade him for one."

"Look, we've missed out on a voice — Tamala's contact; a man from Moscow. It is a pity but it's no big deal. He would be the first link, that's all. Very junior. Christ, man, with the size of their team they don't have to let their top brass answer telephones. You know that better than I do."

"The fact is we don't know what we have missed but from here on we need a phone tap."

"Look, Frits . . ."

"No. I've gone along with you so far but now I have no choice. You've heard the tapes; the ball is back with this character who calls himself Smith. He's not going to walk in the office again and make another speech for us. You heard him today — he was off that line like it was hot. Now he has them biting he'll be a lot more cautious."

"He might not even phone the office."

"Right. That's why we'll also be tailing Tamala and we're going to find out whether your precious Nero is as useful as you think. Maybe he knows a face for this Mr Smith."

"Jesus, you are taking it seriously."

"Hundred percent. Think how this looks from Pretoria: some clown comes off the street into the FAM office and says he has the answer to all their prayers. Tamala soaks it up then runs to his friends from Moscow. They think about it and say — very interesting, we accept your conditions for trying a sample. What sample? Is he laying on a trial run? What the hell are we talking about anyway? Sure I'm taking it seriously. We can't sit on our arses and wait for something to happen." De Wet spoke English with only a trace of the accent that thickened the speech of his deputy but he bit off each word as if he were trying to stop the next one from escaping.

Meester heard him without comment and then said, "So what next?"

"For you? Get on to Nero. Find out if he has anything for us, whether he saw Smith at all. If he did then he ought to have reported in of his own accord, but you'd better go easy or he'll get all defensive and say he knows nothing."

"I know how to handle Nero."

"Sure. If he did see Smith then I think we might show him a few picture books — we'll have to be a bit selective though."

"I'll be careful."

"The only other thing is the phone tap. I want it now, Danny, if not sooner."

The Afrikaner screwed up his big, square face in impatience as well as displeasure. "I don't think he'll do it."

"Try him. Offer him a three month bonus and double the rate for as long as it stays in place. Tell him, one way or another, with or without him, we're tapping that phone."

At the Catford Greyhound Stadium, Meester placed a one pound bet on Harry's Comet. He tucked the slip absently in his pocket and sauntered away from the counter towards a new vantage point near a kiosk. He stood there for a while, waiting and watching until the dogs for the eighth race were being led to the traps, then he moved his position again. His pound was on an even money favourite, running as number five. Meester was not really a gambling man.

He watched the dummy hare streak into view under the powerful lights, shaking mechanically and drawing the dogs to their top speed within seconds. Only then did Meester turn to the small figure who was standing nearby. A West Indian, most whites would have guessed, but nobody was guessing. Above the shouting and barking of the last race Meester delivered his message. When it was over the tote flashed the news that he had lost his pound but by then he was already on his way out.

The house was about fifteen minutes walk from the dog track and by arrangement Meester got there first, letting himself in by the front door and immediately checking all rooms and the outlook to the rear. For about ten minutes he waited behind the faded front curtains and watched for Nero's approach. From the house next door a man emerged and hurried away. The quiet comings and goings of solitary males was accepted and understood by those who lived in the neighbourhood. There would be no suspicions aroused, no explanations needed. Except from directly opposite it would be impossible to distinguish one shadowy doorway from the next. Nero passed suddenly and silently in front of the window and he stepped inside.

They used a room at the back which had the window boarded up and was covered with a square of hardboard for good measure. "Any trouble?" Meester asked.

"No trouble, but this is very inconvenient for me. Tonight I had other things to do. I had to make excuses. It doesn't look good."

"It isn't what I would choose to be doing either, but we haven't heard much from you lately."

"I can't help it if there is nothing new." He gave Meester a sleepy, knowing smile. "I have told you before, if the Free Africa Movement is not moving you should be glad." Lifting an old dining-room chair with one hand he spun it so that he could sit astride and lean on the backrest. "Your places get worse and worse. Why do we have to talk in this dump?"

"It isn't just a chat this time; we need to look at a few pictures."

"What sort of pictures?" He searched his coat pockets for cigarettes.

"Photos of people you haven't told us about, Nero."

The black man stiffened and looked at Meester through half closed eyes. "What are you giving me, man?"

"Tamala had a visitor last Friday. I want to know all about him."

"He gets a lot of visitors."

"He had only one on Friday morning. He sounded educated. English."

Nero blew a smoke ring. "I think I know who you mean. But I never spoke to him. He went straight in to Tamala and straight out again. You should have it all — that's why I look after your damn bug for you."

"Tamala didn't talk to you about him?"

"No."

"Why not?"

"How do I know? He doesn't talk to me about everything."

"Why do you think he didn't?"

Nero shrugged. "Not important. Probably just enquiries, sympathizers, journalists. We get plenty."

"It wasn't that. This one might be an arms dealer."

Nero hesitated. "We get those too. Tamala still doesn't have to talk about it."

"Do you think he suspects you?"

"No way. There is nothing against me except the bug and that goes where I go."

"That's good. Did you get a look at him?"

"I saw him walk in and out."

"Well?"

Nero draped an arm over the chair back and examined a gold cufflink. "Red hair."

"Christ man, this is like drawing teeth. What did he look like?"

"Nothing special. Red hair, very white, a lot taller than me, maybe taller than you. Dress like nothing. Raincoat I think."

Meester sighed and brought over another chair. There was no table in the room. From a very old briefcase he took one of three photograph albums and laid it on the seat. "This could take a long time but it might be worth money to you."

It was through a haze of smoke that Nero picked out two photographs in the third album. He wasn't sure about them — could not possibly be because they were two different people.

"Fantastic," Meester said without enthusiasm, but he produced an impressive wad of notes. "There's a three-month bonus here. It's supposed to be the limit I can go to but I'd rather you just took the whole bloody lot and let's go home to bed. And I want you to stick this in his telephone." In his hand he held a tiny plastic cylinder.

Nero's lips curled back from gleaming white teeth and his eyes opened wide. "*What?*"

"It's going to be done anyway. You might as well get paid for it."

"Bug his phone? Are you crazy?"

"It shouldn't be for long but we have to have his incoming calls. There's no other way."

"Not me. No chance. Twice he's got his comrades to come and do a sweep for him, you know that. When you came up with the last bugging idea you said you weren't expecting anything so stupid. Just something you can put in and out from your side of the wall, you said. No risk of them finding it while you are out. Deactivate it, take it with you, you said. We understand. And now you come up with this! No way."

"We still understand," Meester told him. "But it's going in anyway and if it's found you'll get the same grilling so what's the difference? If you do it for us at least you'll be sure how to take it out if you get half a chance. And you'll make yourself a lot of money. It may only be for a few days. When was the last sweep?"

"Hell of a long time ago."

The Afrikaner scratched his grizzled head. The best course would be to invite a sweep by giving Tamala something to be suspicious about. Once the rooms had been found to be electronically clean again it ought to be safe for a while. But he knew that de Wet would not wait, so he played the last card. "I'll double your rate for every day that it stays in. The way you'll be making money you'll be able to live like a king."

"The way you're talking I'm not going to live at all. I feel like pulling out."

"But you know you can't, not unless you disappear completely. You'll have both sides looking for you, Nero. You've done too much already."

"You are real bastards, you know that?"

"I know."

"If I don't do this you really will break in and do it anyway?"

"Not me, but somebody will that's for sure. That crappy little office of yours is not exactly Fort Knox. A bug or a wire tap won't be any problem, though I'm not the expert on such things. I only know that this is the simplest one to get out in a hurry." He bounced the miniature transmitter in the palm of his hand.

Nero got suddenly to his feet and began to pace about with quick, light steps on his elevator heels. "I want a full year's bonus for this, man. Plus the double rate while the thing stays in. Or I'm running for it."

Meester looked at him appraisingly. "I'll get it for you," he said calmly. "The usual drop. Now here's what you do with this little gadget."

They left separately, and with only a litter of cigarette ends to mark their passing.

TWO

THE PHOTOGRAPHS IN the three thick albums bore only numbers. Names and other details were stored in the computer for fast retrieval and were also in classified files in a section of the archives known as the crypt. Meester had no access to the computer record except through de Wet, or under contingency plans for the event of de Wet's demise or unexpectedly having to 'relinquish his responsibilities'. At eight o'clock next morning, when de Wet arrived at the office, Meester emerged from the crypt feeling none too pleased.

"You check it out," he said flatly, and slapped down a sheet with two scrawled numbers.

"What's the problem?"

"There are only two possibles, I told you that last night. One of them I've ruled out and the other isn't in the bloody files. Try your own records."

"It has to be there. The computer entries are taken from the files, not the other way round."

"Well there's nothing on file now."

De Wet looked irritated rather than puzzled. He picked up the paper and left the room without another word. Meester wondered why he always wore crepe soles. They were out of character. Perhaps it was something to do with his feet.

"Nothing," de Wet admitted when he got back. "Are you sure the other one can be ruled out?"

Meester instantly felt better. "Positive. The one I checked was a *verkrampte* rabble rouser who couldn't talk like an Englishman if he wanted to. And if he had to do a deal with Tamala it would probably give him a stroke." He hefted his briefcase on to his knee and pulled out the album. It flopped open at the marked page and he shoved it across the desk. "There's your mystery man then."

The picture showed a man in his thirties standing between two cars and obviously in conversation with somebody who was off the photograph. The face was unremarkable, rather lean. He wore a coat with toggles and appeared to be tall though there were only the vehicles to set the scale. De Wet frowned at first and then recognition dawned. "This is not from our collection at all, that's why there's no entry against it. There ought to have been a note. I remember giving it to Lottie to file before she left."

"Well, who is he?"

"I don't know but I think we can find out. It was taken by the industrial security people. They sent it to their HQ and industrial liaison sent it to us." Something close to excitement began to show on his face. "You see, it was taken here, in London."

"Who do we ask?"

"That's the problem; I'll have to trace it back the way it came — through Pretoria."

"But that's ridiculous! It could take days."

"I have a feeling they will move fast on this one. In any case, we have no choice. The mines employ dozens of security agents and we need to find the one who took the picture." Even as he spoke de Wet was roughing out a message that he would code and pass to Chris Collins for transmission.

Meester interrupted his writing. "What's the story behind this? Or do I only find out if you drop dead?"

Sarcasm was wasted on de Wet. "We didn't get much background. They just wanted to know if we had anything on him because he'd been associating with somebody they had under surveillance."

"I see. That's not so good. If they are trying to be discreet we're going to blow it all for them."

"Let's hope we don't have to. It's months ago now. Maybe they've finished the case and done the enquiries themselves. Anyway, until we hear from HQ all we can do is sit on that bloody tape recorder and hope your little Nero doesn't fool around with the phone job."

"And hope that Mr Smith, whoever he is, is stupid enough to phone the FAM office again."

"I think we can be sure that Smith will want to keep out of reach so he will phone Tamala, not the other way around. If I am right,

20

there is a chance that it will be at the office or Tamala's apartment."
He returned to his scribbling.

"You'll bug his home phone too?"

This time de Wet replied without looking up. "That, Danny, has already been done."

As soon as his deputy had gone de Wet took the message through to records and found Collins alone at the radio.

"Send this right away, and then I want to talk to you."

Collins did as he was told, wondering what was coming next. De Wet waited, leaning his buttocks against the edge of the table.

When he had finished, Collins pulled off the headset and swivelled round. "Yes, Frits," he said brightly.

De Wet looked at him as if he were trying to guess his weight, then he said, "Tell me, and be honest, what do you think these are?" He waved an arm along the row of tape machines.

Collins only hesitated for a moment. "Everybody knows what they are: they're eavesdroppers."

"Did anybody say so?"

"No, we don't discuss them."

"Then how do you know what they are?"

Collins shrugged his broad young shoulders. "What else could they be?"

"And you imagine that there are all kinds of interesting secrets being recorded do you?"

"No, I don't. I should think that Jutta has to listen to one boring conversation after another, but there must be something useful now and again or we wouldn't keep it up."

"Quite so. In fact, keeping it up has become something of a problem right now. Jutta has more than she can handle which is why I am talking to you about it. I want you to help out."

Collins looked amazed. "But I'm not cleared for that. I mean, I'm not allowed to . . ."

"If I give you responsibilities beyond your level of security clearance that's my problem not yours. I want you to help Jutta."

"Well, of course, if you say so."

"Good. I will tell Jutta and she'll brief you herself on what she needs. I shall inform Pretoria and you will probably have the pleasure of reading their reaction before I do, unless of course they code it."

In the event Pretoria moved quickly on both issues. The agent who had taken the photograph was named as one Charles McLeod who worked for Consolidated Rand. He was still in London. De Wet then received a reprimand for exceeding his responsibilities with regard to Christian Collins. His predicament, however, was appreciated and, yes, he was right in assuming that HQ could not supply him with additional staff at a few hours' notice. Collins's security clearance was now under review. De Wet knew that that would involve weeks of exhaustive enquiries not only into Collins's own background but into the personal histories of his English father and Afrikaner mother as well. Unmoved by the rebuke, de Wet sent his assurance that he would not extend Collins's duties any more than was absolutely necessary for coping with the present alert. He then went personally to meet Charles McLeod.

At the end of the 1960s, when Britain terminated arms sales to South Africa, the Republic retaliated by selling its gold through Zurich rather than the London bullion market. This had extensive repercussions in the finance and insurance houses of several capitals but the trade soon settled down again and began to flow through an even more complex circuitry than before. One small consequence of the upheaval was the complete reorganization of the London offices of Consolidated Rand and subsidiaries. They abandoned their earlier premises and took over a different block of concrete and glass which they called New Rand House near St Giles. The name appeared in stylish lettering on stone above the frontage but it failed to impress de Wet. He thought it looked inappropriate, like a vintage label on a soft drink. He took the lift to the seventh floor and, by appointment, introduced himself to the sectional manager to whom he had spoken on the phone. After a brief exchange the manager 'wheeled him in' as he put it.

Charles McLeod was sipping coffee when they appeared in his doorway and he put his cup down carefully before getting to his feet.

"What can I do for you, Mr de Wet?" The handshake was firm, the smile was friendly. If there was a faint Scots accent it was too subtle for de Wet's foreign ear and nothing else about the little man could be reconciled with what de Wet thought he knew about the Scots.

"Information, Mr McLeod, information."

The other nodded. "Coffee?"

"No thank you, I'm sure you are very busy so I'll come straight to the point. A few months ago you sent a photograph of a man to National Security in Pretoria. You wanted it passed on to the appropriate section for comment. This is the picture."

McLeod examined it for a moment then looked up. "I remember. They couldn't help us."

"So I understand. In fact now they are asking you to help them. They want to follow it up themselves."

"In what connection?"

De Wet spread his hands.

"Did they tell you anything about it? Why I took it?"

"All I know is that it's a picture of somebody who was associating with the person you had under surveillance at the time."

"Hardly that. There was one meeting to my knowledge but it could have been important and I wanted to know who he was because I had few other leads at the time."

"And now?"

"Now it doesn't matter; that chapter is finished."

"Can you tell me about it?"

Charlie McLeod turned to his filing cabinet. "The chief says you're from the embassy and I'm to co-operate with you," he said over his shoulder. "What exactly do you do, Mr de Wet?"

"Admin., mostly. I'm a second secretary."

"But you pass on information to the NIS."

"Embassies can be useful to a lot of ministries, not just the Intelligence Service."

McLeod smiled without parting his lips and came back with a slim folder. "I can imagine. But in this case your value will be limited because I don't know who your man is. You, or they, will have to find out. I can give you a start." He came round the desk and settled himself in another armchair beside de Wet. It was a tiny office but, in McLeod's opinion, more than adequate for someone who disliked offices and didn't spend much time there. "I'm out more than I'm in, you understand. It's a reporter's life, really,

23

without quite so much pressure. On the other hand we never have the satisfaction of seeing our work published."

"Like being a private detective, I should think."

"That sort of thing but in a specialist field. I'm sure that as a good Afrikaner you know that South Africa produces most of the world's gold."

"And gem diamonds."

"Right. But that's another story. Gemstones are a bit like works of art in that they are only worth what people are prepared to pay. The price of gold fluctuates according to supply and demand just like anything else of course, but at any given time the price can be quoted in figures you can depend on. You know that nobody is going to come along with a watchmaker's glass and tell you that your bit of gold is a poor colour or has a flaw on one of its facets, if you follow my meaning."

De Wet did.

"Well now," McLeod went on, "the upshot of this is that gold has much greater potential for enormous quick profits. When gold prices peak, as they did in 1980, the chaps with the biggest reserves can really cash in before the crash comes. And you can be sure that the price will pick up again. You'll never destroy people's faith in gold — it can't be created and there's surprisingly little of it about. As a matter of fact, if all the gold that has ever been mined in the world were to be melted into one great cube it would only be about sixty-five feet across. Did you know that?"

"Really? Is that all? Including all the Inca gold and the ancient . . ."

"All of it. The lot. So you'll appreciate that the production end of the gold business has some pretty competitive technology, and in this field the Soviets are running a very poor second. That's the super-sensitive area from the point of view of security work."

"Safeguarding the latest technology."

"That's right. From prospecting to refining we are in the lead, though the Canadians are damn good too." McLeod lifted his folder as if he were about to reveal something but decided to hold back a little longer. "Employees in sensitive areas are generally screened quite thoroughly but it's impossible to stop every

24

loophole. Whenever there is cause for suspicion about somebody they bring it to the attention of security."

"And you are part of the investigating team."

"Just a small part but being London-based I sometimes get a fairly big slice of the cake on my plate. About a year ago that's what happened. A young research assistant had been involved in some trials on a new process but suddenly lost interest and resigned for no obvious reason. She had been keeping some pretty odd company and it didn't look too good because there had been access to other information that was even more sensitive. The fear was that she'd collected a highly saleable package and done a bunk with it."

"She?"

McLeod gave one of his little smiles and opened his folder. "See for yourself."

The face was well shaped and the expression serious: attractive without being beautiful. Her hair was long and dark and tumbled freely over her shoulders. A CND pendant shone in contrast on the monochrome print. De Wet put her in her late twenties. He took his own photograph and deliberately fitted the two together.

"Oh, they're two halves of the same picture alright," McLeod assured him. "Taken in the car park of a supermarket in Lewisham. They were chatting together for quite a while. It *looked* like a chance meeting and now I think it probably was but at the time I was very curious about the chap. I couldn't ask Diane of course, that's her name — Diane Marsh, because I never got beyond what you might call the, er, covert phase of operations."

"And you decided not to take it any further?"

"Well, I don't take those kind of decisions. Let's just say that on the evidence that I wasn't getting it was decided not to continue. We had nothing on her really. She was in with a trendy, lefty lot at one time but I don't believe she had any contacts that we needed to worry about."

"Is she South African?"

"Born in Cape Town but has a British passport. They are hard ones to keep tabs on if they get the urge to travel."

De Wet said he could believe it. He asked what her particular branch of research had been.

"She was only an assistant, you understand, but she's quite a bright girl and has a degree in chemistry. She was involved in a small-scale separation and refining project but the same laboratories were being used for other research on processing and some of it turned out to be pretty exciting stuff. You probably know that all kinds of by-products are associated with gold mining — uranium for example. It was what she had access to rather than what she was doing that got some people worried."

"What's she doing now?"

"Nursing a baby, I should think. She started doing some sort of course at the local college but got married and pregnant, I'm not sure in which order, and packed it in. She was what you might call great with child last time I saw her."

"What does her husband do?"

"Teaches at the South London Polytechnic. They have a semi in Sydenham."

De Wet became thoughtful. "You say she's quite bright. I'm not sure whether that's good or bad. How co-operative do you think she will be when we ask for information?"

"Well, she won't be eager to help you lot, that's for sure. And your CD plates won't impress her overmuch either." He watched de Wet stroking his little moustache and guessed what was coming next.

"Charles, can I ask you to do this for us? We need a name and address, that's all. We can handle it from there. It probably won't take you more than a couple of hours, but put in for a full day's expenses and there will be no problem. If you can fit it into your own routine that's good but if you want me to clear it with your head of section I'm sure he'll co-operate."

McLeod was doubtful. "I have no more authority for asking questions than you have, you know."

"I realize that, but you are a professional and you don't sound South African either. If we mess it up and she gets stubborn it could lose us valuable time."

"How soon do you want the information?"

"Yesterday. It really is urgent."

"All right. I'll see what I can do but she might get stubborn with me too, y'know. That's a risk you'll just have to take."

"Agreed."

The house was not far off the A212, in a new development called Derwent Close. They were quite successful little dwellings which managed to look neat rather than flimsy. It was a valiant attempt to move away from apartments in an area where space was the most expensive commodity. Diane Marsh waved her hand as her husband drove out on to the main road then she pulled down the up-and-over door to the garage and repositioned their other car, a second-hand mini, in front of it. In wet weather the routine was an unbearable nuisance but today it was fine and faintly sunny. She hurried back towards the sound of the baby's crying and found that the milk, standing in its pan of hot water, had become too hot. She ran the bottle under the tap and shook it vigorously while she jiggled the infant's mattress to try and lessen the screaming.

She had been passionately in favour of breast feeding, especially when she realized how strongly some people disapproved of it in public. But her nipples were retracted, her milk was apparently insufficient and the whole business had been extremely disappointing. Nor had she been demonstrative, lately, about any of her other strong convictions. She was thirty and the antics of British youth had come to seem naive while the people in her own social circle, even those who shared her views, were solidly conservative in the way they behaved. She sprinkled a few drops of milk on her arm, decided it was about right and picked up baby Bryan. The crying stopped instantly and he began to guzzle with a deep concentration.

It was about that time, to her irritation, that she heard a knock at the door. Damn! If it was somebody trying to sell something they could just keep on moving. Cradling Bryan in her arms she went to answer the knock.

"Good morning Mrs Marsh. Don't worry, I'm not trying to sell anything." He raised his hat, smiled gently and got the words out before she could speak. "It is Mrs Marsh isn't it?"

"Yes, that's right but . . ."

"Don't you worry, I'll not bother you for more than two minutes. I'll be on my way before that bonny baby of yours has stopped to draw breath. He withdrew a buff envelope from an inside pocket and slid out a folded, printed form. "All I need, Mrs Marsh, is to see you confirm that Mr Robin Spink here is a person of good character who can be expected to honour his financial obligations and . . ."

"I beg your pardon? Who? Are you sure you've got the right Mrs Marsh?"

The little man seemed to sink inwardly; discouraged but not surprised. He turned his form over and refolded it so that it stiffly displayed a passport sized photograph stuck within a marked square with the caption 'applicant should attach passport photograph here'. "Well, it's the name he's given clearly enough. See — Robin A. Spink — that's what it says, and he's given you as a guarantor — Mrs Diane Marsh of number 9 Derwent Close. See for yourself." He turned the paper so that they could read it together. She had both hands occupied with baby and bottle and at that point the baby found something not to his liking. Perhaps the sun was in his eyes when he opened them. Or perhaps there was an air lock somewhere. Whatever the reason, baby Bryan chose that moment to leave off sucking. Then there was a burp and a dribble of bubbly milk and he started to bawl again. She hefted the infant against her shoulder and rubbed its back while she turned her head to study the facts that were being presented to her. The name of the applicant was clearly typed beneath the signature and it was indeed as the man said. Equally plainly her own name and address appeared as one of two guarantors given in the space above. She was frowning hard as she looked at the photograph. It was only head and shoulders and the head was turned so as to show considerably less than full face. It probably wouldn't have been accepted for a passport. Recognition came swiftly and it took her by surprise.

"He's not called Spink, that's Keith Tyler! He wouldn't give me as a guarantor or anything else."

The man looked quite troubled. "But the address," he said as if in mild protest. "Lomand Street; that's his address isn't it?"

"I've no idea where he lives. I hardly know him. I used to see him occasionally when we lived abroad but I've only set eyes on him once in the last twelve months."

"Abroad? You mean this man is a foreigner?"

"No, he's English but what I'm saying is that I scarcely know

28

him and I'm certainly not guaranteeing him for anything. What's he been . . ."

"Look," he said, as if there was a final point that would settle any confusion. "The fellow you know, what's his occupation?"

"He worked for a chemical firm overseas but I don't know what he's doing now. I tell you, I've only seen him once in the last year. He said he was on an extended holiday."

The man stuffed the form back in his pocket and shook his head with what could have been disappointment, disapproval or disbelief. "I'm very sorry you've been troubled, Mrs Marsh. It just shows you can't be too careful. We get all kinds and we just have to check up on everything. You won't be bothered again I assure you." He touched his hat and turned to go.

"But what has he been trying to do?"

"Best not to be involved in any way, Mrs Marsh," he said over his shoulder. "You know nothing about it and that's the best position for you to be in."

She watched him walk away while baby Bryan continued to scream in her ear. Inside the house she tried to get him back on to his bottle while she cradled him in his favourite position but it was no good. Perhaps he did not like the look on her face.

Tamala's phone began to transmit at about lunchtime so that during the afternoon Collins was able to hear incoming calls as well as conversations which took place in the FAM office. It was towards the end of the working day that, much to his excitement, the voice which he had been so carefully coached to recognize, crackled briefly over the line.

"I've delivered," it said. "Have you collected yet?"

"Yes. No problems."

"Good. Remember, they have to move fast on it, I'll be in touch."

It was not much but Collins, in his youthful enthusiasm, could not shut the voice out of his mind and he thought up half a dozen possible interpretations for what it had said. De Wet had told him almost nothing. In fact, Collins would have been surprised to know that his guesses were worth as much as anybody else's. All the

29

others could do, as they later huddled over the brief transcript, was wonder whether they had missed anything before Nero had had a chance to get at the telephone.

"It's possible, of course, that they already had plans for the drop," de Wet pointed out. "In any case, we now have surveillance on Tamala so, if he did collect anything, he must have been very clever about it. It seems more likely that his friends collected direct and then confirmed with Tamala. It's the confirmation that we've missed."

Meester shrugged. "A word or a sign in the street would have been enough."

"Exactly. His big comrades are not amateurs even if our Mr Smith seems to be."

"Smith or Tyler. I still think we could have got more out of that Marsh woman."

"I did not ask for more, Danny. I said the name and address would be enough. If McLeod says she had no address then we must accept that. The important thing is that we now have a name and we know that he's English and spent some time in South Africa. That has to be so because Mrs Marsh has never lived anywhere else outside the UK. He's a possible and the only one we've got, so it still has to be followed up. Either we rule him out or we run him down. To start off with it's the same procedure. I only wish I could do it myself."

"So do I," Jutta Keiner put in wistfully. But that evening it was Danny Meester who climbed aboard the SAA 747 bound for Cape Town.

THREE

FRITS DE WET had not the slightest doubt that, in all matters of a technical nature, the Free Africa Movement would turn to Moscow for advice. He would never have taken seriously the sort of claims put forward by the man calling himself Smith had he not firmly believed that Russian advisers had found them interesting. In this belief de Wet had been right and, while Danny Meester was in South Africa compiling his dossier on one Keith Tyler, certain related events were taking place in an obscure settlement six thousand miles to the north. The place was called Tarka and was marked by one of a cluster of pins in the distribution maps for correctional labour camps.

It was a relatively small camp, Tarka, less than two hundred men and specially set up to provide work gangs for the new line to the Taz mining complex. It was a temporary camp, a camp without tradition or reputation whose prisoners were all destined to be transferred when the work was finished. All would remain under a strict regime of correctional labour for the duration of their sentences. Most would be returned to big, permanent camps with high ranking staff. Some might be redeployed in temporary establishments like Tarka where the officer in charge, despite his years of service, was still only a senior lieutenant.

Cherdyn was his name and, irrespective of his rank, Lieutenant Cherdyn could count on being treated with a certain respect in any company. He wore the blue collar tabs and shoulder boards of the uniformed KGB. In turn he paid virtual homage to his own superiors and he was particularly deferential that night on the telephone. The unexpected call came from his directorate headquarters in Moscow and the caller was the equivalent of a full colonel.

"Yes, sir," Cherdyn said at attention. "Speaking sir."

"I have just been reading your monthly return. It is most concise."

Cherdyn had no idea that the routine reports ever reached such levels in head office. He tried anxiously to remember what he had written in his most recent effort. Nothing of any consequence, surely. The returns were just a formality; an irritation in which something had to be put down under a dozen standard headings every month. The last ore had been as humdrum as the rest. "Yes sir. Thank you sir."

"This Kazakh — what's the name — Oleg Bykov. Are you still having trouble with him?"

Cherdyn frowned. "We are not having any trouble, colonel. We have him quiet now, in solitary confinement. If he gets violent again I will soon . . ."

"But he is a nuisance. Has he ever been any use to you out there?"

"It is true that we have not been able to use him properly. He cannot work with the others."

"Then have him ready to fly out on Wednesday morning. Eleven hundred hours. Tell the *feldsher* to have him sedated, thoroughly. You will be well rid of him."

"Yes sir." Cherdyn knew better than to ask questions.

"Eleven hundred hours on Wednesday. It will be one of ours."

The lieutenant shook his head when he replaced the handset. The crazy Kazakh was to be *flown* out, on a *Komitet* aircraft! Nobody would believe it.

"Flying out!" the *feldsher* echoed. "Where to?"

"What does it matter," Cherdyn snapped. "The further the better. It doesn't make any difference. Just make sure he's thoroughly sedated, that's all. And it's all I need to report on," he added pointedly.

The paramedic felt vaguely annoyed with himself for having been caught off guard and giving Cherdyn the pleasure of showing his teeth. "I shall need help if I have to give an injection to that ape," he said.

The lieutenant turned away. "Just dope him. It's up to you."

The solitude was not in itself a burden to Bykov, he could take it with a shrug. Being separated from the others was better, really, than being forced to listen to their stupid talk. But the guards knew that and because they knew they tried to make the physical

32

suffering even worse. He hoped he had killed Klenko; hoped that his big, gaping lolling mouth would never talk again. *You didn't need to keep hitting him. Why did you keep on hitting him?* Stupid, all of them. If the others hadn't dragged him off he would have smashed the face out of existence. At the thought his massive fists, shaking spasmodically, bunched tighter and he bit hard into the chewed-up folds of the blanket.

It would be dark soon. They would have to give him more blankets then or he would not live through the night. Perhaps that was what they intended. He had seen men die from cold. They stopped shivering towards the end and just went to sleep as if their bodies had given up trying to keep warm. Was it their bodies or their minds that gave up? Did they lose the will or did they just become numb and feel nothing? How would it be?

The wind had dropped. No rattles, no singing from the wires. It would freeze all the harder until the straight wires became so brittle they would snap if you twisted a stick in them. But you couldn't break the coils like that; you couldn't lever your way through the tangle of loose rolls, and the dogs would hear you if you tried. They'd be curled up in their boxes now in the no-man's-land between the first two fences, but they'd hear and would tear the throat from any man who came crawling through the coils. The guards would have no need to shoot. No way over, no way through and, in the rock-hard ground of the permafrost, no way under.

It was more than an hour before they came. He heard the muffled thumping of boots on packed snow and saw a pattern of chinks around the door as a searchlight settled over the block. There was no longer any light from a slit window high in the opposite wall. He felt, as well as heard, heavy footsteps on the raised planking outside the door then thick bolts were drawn and smaller bolts snapped back and forth in two rifles as the door swung open and light beamed into the log-built cell.

He remained on his side against the far wall, hugging his knees to his chest. The blanket was gathered around him and drawn up like a purse, held shut by clenched teeth and fists. Only his eyes moved as he stared back at the figures in the doorway — two bulky silhouettes. They didn't say anything; they never spoke to prisoners in solitary. One carried a bundle which he tossed to the floor; there was no bunk or other furniture in the cell. For several seconds more they stared at him, then turned their heads to each other and nodded. One of them slammed the door and the bolts were slid back. Footsteps retreated and after a while the chinks of light disappeared. The statutory four blankets had been provided for the hours of darkness. The prisoner would survive the night or, if he didn't, they would not be held to blame.

He eased his back away from the wall and dragged himself towards the bundle, one hand held stiffly in front of him. Finding the cloths he cradled them against his side, dully aware of their different smell as he made his way along the wall to the corner. He removed a fistful of rags from a circular hole in the floor and after much fumbling his urine poured on to a little pile of frozen excrement beneath. When he had finished he pushed the rags back into the palely glowing hole to keep out the cold. It was the one advantage of the northern camps, the lavatory arrangement. You carried the sewage away on a shovel from beneath the raised floors. Further south, where they tried to use drains, it was always worse.

Bykov did not sleep that night, nor had he slept on the nine previous nights. Through the black, freezing hours he fought the cold and when dawn came he lay aching and exhausted. The first meal of the day was brought to him about an hour after sunrise. It was always bean soup with bread. There was never enough and more often than not it was cold but sometimes it tasted good because it had been left over in the kitchen and not specially made for the solitary block. On the Wednesday morning, April 15, the soup was well-seasoned and lukewarm. He gulped at it with the bowl to his lips to capture the warmth while it lasted, saving just enough to eat with the bread and wiping up the last trace of nourishment. When he had finished he lay opposite the slit window to wait for the brief time when the sun's rays would pass over him. When the guards came to check up on him before eleven o'clock he was sleeping.

There might have been warmth in the spring sunshine but the wind began again; sighing across the tundra from the North Siberian Plains so that, despite its brightness, the sun was as cold as a diamond. It was a monotonous wind which numbed and killed inexorably, purging all life of the weak and injured. Among the wild things of the tundra, only the perfect would survive. The labour gangs protected themselves as best they could, wearing all they possessed and wrapping their shaven heads until they squinted and breathed through ice-rimmed slits. There was little talk between them during their four-hour shifts. The work needed no discussion. Machinery had opened up the route seasons before. Machinery had cut and levelled the track bed, and heavy trucks, burning specially refined fuel in insulated tanks had left dumps of rails and sleepers. The dumps and beds now had to be cleared of snow and the sleepers and rails had to be manhandled into position ready for the engineers who would come in the summer. They would come as volunteers for the long rouble — bonus pay which boosted earnings by more than 50 per cent. Time was money and convicts could save both.

Once laid, the tracks would stay firm until an exceptional summer melted the surface soil. In slightly warmer regions this happened every year and though the ground would still be frozen to a depth of a thousand feet the surface would be a quagmire and an engineer's nightmare. Everything had to be set on deeply-driven piles if it was to stay upright. Even around Tarka the buildings were set on short stilts to stop them melting their way into the ground by their own warmth.

But permafrost technology held no interest for the work gangs as they heaved and slipped and struggled through their shifts. Their lives were as harsh and constant as the wind that tormented them. On the nights that they thawed and stank through the political lectures they were told of their role in building the nation, of Siberia's vast mineral wealth that was the envy of the world, of gold, diamonds and minerals of great strategic importance which would be used in the defence of the motherland. But their eyes remained dull, their minds occupied, if at all, by intensely personal matters: friends, enemies, hunger, new failings they had noticed in their bodies. Survival. Not one thought of the man from Kazakh-stan who had the strength of an ox and the tantrums of a child.

The Ilyushin arrived at 11.20, buzzing the strip once to check on the state of the surface, the pilot trusting nobody. The windsock pointed doggedly southwards and the grey, twin engined plane banked in a wide arc to begin its final approach into the wind. From the main camp a hundred faces followed its course while at the airstrip a knot of guards and trusties gathered outside the hut which served as a waiting-room, avgas store and cargo shed. It was Lieutenant Cherdyn's intention to join them there; to be the first to meet whoever might be on the plane and to have the prisoner brought from the hut, ready for boarding the very moment he was required. As the plane touched down, however, the prisoner was still being chivvied, kicked and half carried from his cell. Two guards had blood at the mouth and nose and Bykov had already paid dearly for it. He scarcely felt his injuries, though, as he stumbled and lurched towards the airstrip in a crush of greatcoats and rifle butts. His big head lolled and jerked above them but the eyes in that haggard face saw little beyond the blur of guards and snow. He wasn't struggling any more and if they had left him alone he would probably have fallen.

The plane swung round at the end of the strip and taxied back to the hut. The engines shuddered to a halt and two trusties promptly rolled forward a drum of fuel leaving a broad stripe across the snow. A guard carried a hand-pump and another went to attend to the steps and the passenger door. Two men stepped down, both wearing thick coats and chapkas. No uniforms. Cherdyn arrived, breathless, and introduced himself. The two nodded and they went to stand beside the hut, out of the wind. One handed Cherdyn an envelope from an inside pocket. It was an order from Moscow to release Bykov into the custody of the bearer. The signature was that of Cherdyn's Director of Operations. The lieutenant glanced at the expressionless faces and turned to see the progress of the prisoner and escort. They had left the compound and were crossing open ground to the airstrip. He looked away, towards the pilot who was supervising the refuelling. They were not ready to leave yet. The prisoner would be ready as soon as they were. He gestured to the door and tried to smile: "I have a flask," he ventured. "While we are waiting." Their faces unfroze slightly but they refused and one of them began to pace about and stamp his feet.

"You have far to go?" Cherdyn tried next. But at that the other one turned away, shrugging deeper into his coat.

"Far enough," Cherdyn heard him say. And he knew better than to persist.

Bykov had to be helped up the steps of the aircraft but he didn't resist. They settled him at the back and hand-cuffed him to the seat frame. On the opposite side and a little further forward another prisoner sat hunched and motionless. Cherdyn looked again at his copy of the release order. It covered him but told him nothing. He watched the pilot hurriedly sign the fuel docket and climb back into his cockpit, anxious to be away. The two escort men also seemed relieved as they shook Cherdyn's hand in a brief farewell. He watched the Ilyushin climb steeply and noted, as did many others, that it was on a course which led to only one major city — Novosibirsk.

The lieutenant watched until the plane was almost out of sight. A guard approached him, rather sheepishly. He carried a sack, tied at the neck with string and dangling a label. Cherdyn listened to a few words then waved the man away with a click of annoyance. The guard left slightly more smartly than he had arrived — still carrying Bykov's personal effects. By then the Ilyushin was just a solitary speck in the sky and the Kazakh was fast asleep.

A day or two later, at Moscow's Domodedovo airport, a chauffeured limousine drew up squarely in the restricted area in front of the departure doors and three elderly men climbed out. White collar Muscovites they clearly were but beyond that there were no clues. Fazil Beriya, the oldest of the three by a few years, carried a small suitcase and a briefcase in one hand while he felt for his pass with the other. Max Kulik and Mikhail Suslov, carrying equally light luggage, hurried after him. They were late for their flight.

Beriya marched towards the check-in with his enormous head thrust forward, bobbing slightly in time with his step. His nickname was The Horse and he was content to think that it was only on account of his size. He showed his pass and pushed ahead without so much as a glance to check reactions. Doors opened and they were ushered to the aircraft.

To nobody's surprise the world's biggest airline was half an hour late in announcing the flight's departure. There was no apology or explanation offered and only the very first of the travellers to file aboard the plane from the departure lounge could have noticed that three passengers had already been installed. Otherwise, there was

37

nothing to indicate that three names on the manifest had been distinguished with a red priority mark.

The flight was direct as far as Omsk and ground time there was brief. After 45 minutes they were airborne again, following the course of the trans-Siberian railway along the southern edge of the taiga swamp. The flat monotony of conifers and birch was broken only by countless pools and waterways — iced and snow-covered for more than half the year. It was nearly an hour before they began to descend again, this time towards a low plateau, dissected by ravines and watered by the Ob River. In the full light of early afternoon a thousand square kilometres of water shimmered in a great dam while a few miles to the north a pall of smoke obscured the vast industrial complex which it served. Suslov squirmed in his seatbelt and muttered something to Kulik who leaned over for a better view and grunted a few words in reply. He had seen it all before. But even those who had never travelled east of Moscow had read and heard the figures too many times to be entirely ignorant of the size and importance of the Kuzmin steelworks, the tin smelter and the refinery which processed all the gold mined in Siberia. Allowing for political propaganda, Novosibirsk was still a big league city — the eighth biggest in the Soviet Union.

The man who met them on arrival showed no pleasure in it.

"My instructions are to take you first to the office." It was a simple statement, they could take it or leave it.

Beriya nodded without looking at the other two. A black Volga was waiting and the chauffeur didn't need to be told where to go. Speeding through the maze of high-rise apartment blocks he brought them on to Krasny Prospect close to Kalinin Square. From there it was a short distance to a massive grey granite building which was the political nerve centre for Western Siberia. The building itself was a legacy of the Stalin era but the dish antenna, for direct contact with Moscow by communication satellite, was only one of many recent installations. The escort lowered his window and the guard waved them through the main gates, bending at the waist to peer at the others as they passed.

They were led through heavy doors into what might have been the foyer of a very old hotel. But it clearly wasn't. A wide stone stair without carpeting had been sealed off at the first landing and the only other way ahead was guarded by a uniformed 'commissionaire' who carried a submachine gun. From a point close to the ceiling the eye of a closed television circuit stared down indiscriminately. A broad counter was manned by two partially uniformed men, both of whom had 9mm hand-guns in buttoned down holsters on their belts. The escort produced his pass and unfastened his coat. "It's still too warm in here," he remarked. But there was no rejoinder. The two behind the counter were watching the strangers delving for their own papers.

Kulik and Suslov presented the standard Soviet citizens' identity document — a fourteen page personal history which served as an internal passport. Each was stamped with a residence permit — a *propiska* — which authorized the holder to live in Moscow. Visits to Novosibirsk had been registered so the travellers would be permitted to stay in the city for more than three days if they needed to. But they would not be allowed past the desk for three seconds without another, very specific, permit. Suslov's was not there.

"*Spravka?*"

Suslov fumbled about again and produced a small red booklet with the missing *spravka* folded inside it. "Here, in my work pass." The other nodded and registered the details in the computer against the date and time. Beriya offered a quite different and much smaller document in a leather folder and nothing was said. All the papers were then pigeon-holed and the three were each provided with a plastic building pass for the duration of their visit. The commissionaire, although he had just seen the passes given out, examined them one by one before he opened his door to the men from Moscow.

They walked two abreast, Kulik and Suslov behind.

"You had me worried back there. I thought you had come without a *spravka*," Kulik said lightly.

Suslov shrugged. "How could I?" He kept his eyes on the numbered office doors they were passing. His hands were clasped behind his back. "Papers," he muttered.

They waited in a vast hall of a room with rows of solemn-faced typists while the escort made a brief call on an internal phone. "Third floor," he told them at the end of it. "We have to see the major." They trooped out again, their footsteps echoing on the smooth marble.

The major was a slight man in an imported blue suit. He smiled professionally at Beriya and murmured politenesses at the others before ushering the Horse into his inner office and closing the door in their faces. "This is very irregular," he said once they were inside. "I hope there is a good explanation."

Beriya shook his enormous head. "I was hoping you might be able to tell me. You are supposed to be directing operations at this end."

The major snorted and threw up a hand in an oddly French gesture. "I have made the arrangements for you according to this," and he snatched up a typewritten sheet with a long coded telex message stapled to it. "But for what? And who takes responsibility?"

Beriya looked down at him with understanding. "I don't know who they will blame," he said. "You, me, both of us. Perhaps there will be a big party. We are in the same boat but I can see that you have to do more of the rowing. My brief is just to make detailed observations and submit a report direct to the Centre."

"Who at the Centre?" the major demanded.

Beriya lowered his eyes to the letter which the other was still holding. "Comrade Shenkov is signing the orders but as he is not a technical man I do not expect to be reporting to him. Probably he will refer me to somebody else. I am sure he has his own instructions."

The major drew a deep breath and released it very slowly. "I'm sure he has," he sighed. Then he jerked his chin towards the door. "Where do they fit in?"

"Kulik and Suslov? Consultants. Professor Kulik is now with the Brezhnev Academy. He's supposed to be a top man in his field. We've used him before, I think. More than once. Doctor Suslov is from the Ivanovsky Institute but I don't know much about him. They will both submit their reports to me and they know better than to ask questions."

"This was copied to you." The major jerked the papers he held. "Can you add anything? Anything at all?"

The Horse shook its head. "With a classification like that they wouldn't tell me even that much if they could avoid it."

"It's crazy!" The major's voice rose. "I am asked to set this up; to have prisoners ferried, escorted, accommodated, a whole emergency exercise laid on and I don't even know for how long let alone why."

"And I, comrade," Beriya said steadily, "have been ordered down here to make examinations and submit a full report. Until I see what I'm supposed to report on I don't know how long it will take either. I understand, though, that we are to be accommodated."

The major turned abruptly to his desk. "That is the least of our problems." He took an envelope from a drawer. "This is your copy of the letter which has already been sent. You will receive full cooperation. My concern, you understand, is for efficiency. I am annoyed because it is difficult to do this sort of thing properly without a full brief."

Beriya said he quite understood.

The two consultants were sipping strong tea when Beriya rejoined them and they were content to wait a little longer until the escort came back. "It isn't more than half an hour's drive," he told them when he finally showed up. "We have plenty of time."

And so it proved to be. The road was busy but wide, and completely cleared of snow. It ran south along the shore of the great reservoir which the city depended on for half a million kilowatts of electricity and much of its recreation. After the winter sports there would be boating and fishing and then no *dacha*, however humble, would be left empty over a weekend. If the family was not using it there would be friends of family, or friends of friends. Suslov wondered where they all tucked themselves away, for they had scarcely drawn clear of the sprawling city, it seemed, when they were entering the satellite town of Akademgorodok. It was unique, not only in the Soviet Union, but in the world, they had been told. The entire town had been created specially to meet the needs of the Soviet Academy of Sciences which employed nearly twenty thousand people in twenty separate institutions. They passed the famous boarding-school for gifted children that they were always showing on television. Soviet brains, like Russian athletes, were picked out early in life.

Suslov began to think about his own children. They were not high flyers but both were doing well enough at University and it was largely thanks to his own position and influence that they were there. His record was professionally sound and politically spotless. It must remain so, whatever he might think privately about the system. *The system*. What new demands had come out of it now? Why was his 'professional service' suddenly so special that strange doors were being opened to him and he was being taken to places that he was forbidden even to speak of? Perhaps it was nothing important, he reasoned. Perhaps when you worked for *them* you were always clamped under a cover of top secrecy. It was probably just a routine they never changed — like the slogans. On his right the high rise laboratories of the Institute for Natural Compounds towered, cold and grey, above the trees. Even here, he reflected, in a town specially created to promote co-operation between the scientific disciplines, there would be no technical discussions over the telephone, no publication of any research papers without permission from *them*. What could it be like where they were taking him now?

Oleg Bykov blinked with lazy eyes and grinned stupidly. He had given up trying to comprehend but had found the new warmth and comfort irresistible. He had no idea where he was and could barely remember the plane journey. In fact he would have dismissed it as a dream were it not for the fact that he was now, indisputably, a long way from Tarka camp. Also, the others had spoken of plane journeys. He could remember the others clearly; actually see them in the green room and hear their voices as if he were watching a film show over and over again. The one who called himself Vadim had done most of the talking.

"Are you both Kazakhs?"

"Yes."

"Yes."

"Then why are you so big and you so small? Don't they grow people to standard size in Kazakhstan? Are your women all giants and midgets as well?" Then that silly giggle, as if he was drunk.

"Hey you! Where are you from?"

That was to the *chermonazy* who just kept rubbing at his teeth with a bit of stick.

"Well, comrade? Where are you from?"

"The best country in Africa. Where are *you* from?"

"Me? I'm from Georgia; from Tbilisi. I thought you would know that. We Georgians are very well known." More giggling. "They brought me here by air from Svirk — that's near Irkutsk."

"You should have stayed in Georgia, my friend."

"And you should have stayed in Africa. What are you doing here anyway?"

There was a long pause. "I suppose I am here because I once taught one of your Moscow whores a lesson. She talked too much — like you."

"There are no whores in Moscow, haven't you heard? Definitely no Russian whores — that's official."

"Why have they brought us here?" the other Kazakh asked.

"Not just us, I can tell you that. There are others. All from camps I think."

"But why?"

"Who knows why."

"What is this place anyway? Where are we?"

"They don't want us to know. They brought two of us from a military airstrip in a van without windows. Does anybody know?" Nobody did.

"I'm scared."

Bykov heard his own voice then. "I don't give a shit. At least it's warm."

"There are women here, did you know that?"

"With us, you mean?"

"No, running the place."

"I didn't see any. I'm not interested either."

"When did you get here?"

"Yesterday sometime. I'm not sure. I've been asleep. The bastards gave me a needle."

"Me too."

"It seems like we all got the same treatment."

The door opened then and the guards came in. Bykov saw their faces just as clearly as he recalled their voices. "Hands on your heads. Now you — outside! Move! Move!"

★

43

". . . move? Can you move?"

Bykov tried to raise a hand but something was holding it. The woman's face was less clear than the pictures in his mind and her voice sounded unreal, like a radio. She had a good face though, with beautiful soft lips and he could see as well as hear that she was asking him to move. She brought her face very close when she said it and he was sure he was smiling at her but her expression did not change.

"Can you touch my hand?"

He lifted his head and blinked at the oddly coloured hand with its wiggling fingers. There were no fingernails. His head lolled sideways and he was aware that the hand was attached to an arm that had normal flesh tones but was strangely misshapen and shiny. He felt no pain now and wanted to laugh but was disturbed by the low moaning sound that seemed to come from himself. The woman did not appear to notice it. Her expression stayed the same; she just kept staring at him through the soft glass. He wondered if he could break open the bottle and get her out. Her face turned away then and the radio said:

"Exactly the same pattern; longer but the phases and sequence are the same."

He wanted her face to come close again but the glass began to bend and stretch and it pushed her further from him. He closed his eyes and saw and heard once more the man from Tbilisi but the images were less distinct, the voices further away and getting fainter.

The woman withdrew her arm from the thick plastic sleeve and eased her hand from the moulded glove. Her eyes did not leave the instrument panels. Above the isolation chamber a series of recessed dials showed the temperature, humidity and a slightly reduced air pressure inside. A monitor confirmed that the air filtration system was removing particles down to a hundredth of a micron. Thin leads from Bykov's prostrate body recorded pulse, respiration and skin conductivity. On an EEG machine the tracer needle kicked spasmodically and then traced an unsteady course across its drum. "Exactly the same pattern," she said again.

Behind her Beriya nodded as he murmured into a tiny tape recorder. In the darkness, aside from the light of the chamber, Kulik and Suslov exchanged glances but said nothing. The EEG began to trace an unswerving path and the pulse and respiration monitors ceased to show any activity. The woman started to open the outer section of the double seal which would permit Suslov to introduce his instruments. Slowly he came forward carrying a small tray, gleaming with glass and stainless steel. He handed it to the woman and slipped his hands into the plastic sleeves.

There had been another fall of snow in Moscow when they got back: one of those light, spring falls that turn to slush and tease those who wait impatiently for summer. They did not meet again for several days and when they did it was in a huge complex of modern offices just outside Moscow's ring road.

The three were called together by a man who became known to Kulik and Suslov only as the Colonel. He received them one blustery, sleeting morning in a small conference-room on the ground floor of one of the outlying buildings. It stank of stale ashtrays.

To open the proceedings the Colonel gathered together a number of sheets from an otherwise empty desk and Suslov noticed that his report, which had been demanded as a single hand-written copy, was now in typescript. "You will appreciate," the Colonel began, "that in safeguarding the security of the state we sometimes have to do some very unpleasant work."

"Of course."

"Inevitably."

"You will also appreciate" he said to Kulik and Suslov, "that such work is normally carried out by our own personnel who have accepted at the outset that their duties may involve some distasteful operations. Every policeman in the world must accept that possibility."

"Yes, indeed."

"In this case you were called upon to help because each of you has specialist knowledge in an extremely narrow field. I want you to understand that, of necessity, we have had to involve you in a most exceptional and serious matter of state security."

There was an exchange of swift glances and Beriya nodded his huge head very slowly in an attempt to indicate a deeper knowledge by showing considered agreement.

"I have also decided to tell you something that Comrade Beriya

45

was forbidden to mention." There was more nodding from The Horse but the two consultants remained still and suddenly tense. "This, this obscenity," he intoned as he waved the collected reports, "was obtained for us through the diligence of one of our agents in the west. It has been developed in a western laboratory and your guess is as good as mine as to why they should want such a thing. For our part, our most valuable secret is that we *know*." Again he fixed on the two outsiders. "Comrades, we may need your help in future but until that time your most valuable contribution is your silence. Make no mistake, you are guarding this secret with your lives."

They could take that whichever way they liked, the colonel thought afterwards. But he need not have worried. Kulik had never trusted anybody in his life and when Suslov got home that night, though he was deeply disturbed, he said nothing to his family. His wife never knew that he had so much as visited that vast office complex off Moscow's ring road.

FOUR

Danny Meester's news from South Africa was, in a word, inconclusive. "If Keith Tyler turns out to be our Mr Smith I'll not be surprised," he declared. "But if it's not him that won't amaze me either."

De Wet picked up the two sheets and studied them, one in each hand. "Born Cheshire," he read aloud. "Now aged thirty. Worked as a lab assistant in Manchester . . . got a diploma in chemistry by night school and day release study. Spent two years in the Republic working for Pharmatech." De Wet muttered rapidly through the details supplied by immigration and employment records, but they offered no insight into the man's character. "What about the people he worked with?"

"I spent a morning at Pharmatech," Meester told him. "Tyler's supervisor died a few months ago. Those above him hadn't much personal contact down at Tyler's level. Tyler doesn't seem to have had any workmates as such. His colleagues, the ones I met, said he was the aloof type but they were all Afrikaners . . . you know how it can be."

"He must have had *some* friends over there."

"They couldn't put me on to any. If I'd had a couple of days . . ."

"Couldn't spare you. We have to let them do that kind of follow-up at their end." He returned to his reading but looked up again almost at once. "This could be a corpse we are looking at. Eyes grey, hair red, no distinguishing marks — what the hell does he *do*? Does he go to whore-houses, old churches, trout-streams? It says here fond of music and recreational reading — where did that come from?"

"One of his application forms."

"But what does he read? Karl Marx or Agatha Christie?" He didn't wait for an answer. "I know, you got what you could in the

47

time. It's just a pity you couldn't get more from Pharmatech. Let's hope the English address is still good."

Keith Tyler had left only one forwarding address when he returned to England and that was nearly two years ago. It was the home of his mother who lived near Stoke on Trent. The only other leads were the references that he had supplied to his employers. But, in Meester's opinion, unless he had deliberately tried to cover his tracks he ought not to be too difficult to find. On that reasoning, searching for Tyler would be instructive in itself: the harder it proved to be — the more likely he was to be their man.

In the event it took only two minutes to discover that if Keith Tyler's mother knew the whereabouts of her son she was not about to say so. "Never even bothers to visit me these days," she complained over the phone. And "somewhere down south", was all de Wet could get out of her on the basis of an old friend's enquiry.

"We'll have it checked out of course," de Wet told the others. "Along with everything else."

"Through an agency?" Jutta sounded doubtful.

"Why not? They can be hired to report all progress and stop short of actual contact if they locate him. We will take over before that if it looks like anybody's getting close."

De Wet's shortage of staff was a chronic complaint, but he had a substantial operating fund and he was expected to use it. Through the fieldmen which Meester ran he could mount a small-scale enquiry or surveillance operation, but the job of finding Keith Tyler looked like being a straightforward missing person case. Assignments like that could be lengthy and were bread and butter to private enquiry agencies. The better ones employed some excellent legmen, more than half of them ex-policemen who could do a very professional job for clients who were not too worried about the bill. It was understood that diplomatic missions, like certain corporate bodies in the public eye, often liked to front up individuals as clients. The agencies were more than content with the arrangement as long as the payments came smoothly.

Among Meester's gleanings from South Africa were two more photographs. They were a few years old but showed full face. He arranged another meeting with Nero and took the pictures along together with McLeod's original. Nero was less than enthralled and gave them only a cursory glance.

"I've said I think that's the guy. Now how much longer do you need that damn thing in the phone? It's giving me ulcers, man."

"It's giving you better pay than you've ever had in your life and that's about all it is giving so far. I'll be as glad as you when it's out."

"When?"

"A few more days I should think. You are not helping to speed things up; I need to know which of these pictures is the best — most like the man you saw." Meester merely wanted reassurance that in full face Tyler would still strike the right notes in Nero's memory.

Nero blew out smoke with a hissing sigh. "I don't know. I still see him like this one but maybe in my mind I see the picture now not the man. The new photos don't help."

It was Meester's turn to sigh. "Okay Nero, just sit tight. And keep your eyes and ears open. All we're getting from Tamala's phone is bar talk."

Because they met infrequently the two used the opportunity to discuss more routine things but they were together for only about a quarter of an hour. On his way home to bed Meester worried anew about the telephone. Nero was frightened and not without reason. That in itself was bad. Tamala would know Nero well enough to recognize nervousness even if it came out as bravado. He might already be suspicious, could even be having Nero watched, could be asking for another electronic sweep of his office. If Nero were to be uncovered the setback would be total. London's FAM base would get a complete shakeout and Moscow would be only too happy to help with new security arrangements. Was it worth the risk? Meester had to admit to himself that there was no other way. Young Chris Collins had already picked up the voice again —asking for news. There had been none, but it was enough to prove that Smith was still calling Tamala on his office phone. De Wet had tried not to look smug about it. If they located Tyler and he turned out not to be Smith then the phone would remain their only link. They might not even find Tyler.

By the following afternoon they had learned that the address near Stoke was a fairly new unit in a row of what were now being called town houses, and that Mrs Tyler was apparently living there alone.

Her husband had died when Tyler was seventeen. The agency reported that they were following two leads from Tyler's last British employer but the person most likely to know his present whereabouts was holidaying in Spain and had only just left. They were 'pursuing other possibilities' and would report again the next day.

At about the same time Smith himself called Tamala's office once more to ask for news. This time his impatience forced a few extra words from him.

"But they've had more than enough time now," he protested. "What's the matter with them?"

"We must be patient," Tamala began, but the other rang off.

It wasn't much but it told the listeners that, in Smith's opinion, his offering should by now have been evaluated.

"It probably has been," de Wet remarked. "But they won't rush to say so. Right now they are probably deciding how to handle it — and Mr Smith."

And de Wet was right. But decisions were reached in Moscow that very night and when, a day later, Smith called for news, it was an excited Tamala who answered the phone.

"Yes, there has been a very pleasing development. I think you have won your order."

"As arranged then? Same day, place and time?"

"I have to tell you it won't just be me. They want a meeting."

"That wasn't part of the deal." Smith's voice rose.

"I told them that. But we must see their point of view. Don't worry, we are on the same side. Please be there. Hello? Hello?"

Collins, who had been unconsciously holding his breath, listened to the click of the receiver and released his air like a burst tyre. By now he knew full well whose phone he was listening to. He had been told virtually nothing about the operation but the thing was obviously big and he alone now knew that it was about to take off. He felt a sort of elation which, in his job, was a new experience. As instructed, he listened for a further three minutes in case there was a follow-up call and then, consumed with curiosity, he took the tape to Jutta although he knew that she would tell him nothing.

★

"It's an emergency," de Wet declared later. "Which means that we decide what to do and tell Pretoria afterwards." The 'we' did not go unnoticed by Jutta or Meester and through that mental computer which, unbidden, monitors all human interchange, they understood. De Wet was about to shoulder a major responsibility so his ego could afford to share the decision-making process.

"The main problem," Jutta observed, "is that we are not *sure* of anything. If we read it right then the deadline is tomorrow afternoon — Thursday. But 'same day, place and time' might not mean a repeat of that Thursday stroll out of Tamala's office. It just happens to be the only one we know about. 'As arranged' could refer to an entirely different plan."

"Whenever it is, Tamala will have to go along to make the introduction. It seems pretty certain that he's the only one who has actually seen Smith. Danny has four men keeping a 24 hour watch on Tamala's movements and so far he hasn't met anybody looking like Smith — or what we think Smith looks like." De Wet flashed a sceptical glance without aiming it directly at Meester. "It isn't likely that on their first meeting they would have made arrangements this far ahead and we believe we have heard all their subsequent talk."

"He's been in touch with the Reds somehow," Jutta pointed out.

"Maybe from a phone box. But in any case, the procedure for us has to be the same: we stay with Tamala until he leads us to Smith."

"Then what?" Meester was staring into space.

"That's what we have to decide. What we've just heard changes everything."

"Russians in the next act."

"For sure, Jutta. If we could have located Smith earlier we might have learned who he is, what he is and who he represents. The threat could have been assessed and we could have acted accordingly. If Tamala had led us to him earlier we might still have had time to stop him quietly without things getting out of hand. But now, unless the enquiry people work a miracle, we're not going to see our man until he goes to the party." De Wet allowed himself a smirk at his accidental choice of words but it quickly disappeared and he shook his head. "We can't let things go beyond that point."

Meester and Jutta Keiner glanced at each other.

"You mean . . ."

"I mean what I say; we can't stand by in ignorance and let them go ahead. They have arranged a meeting maybe for tomorrow. Somehow we must make the most of the opportunity; we may not get another."

Jutta thought aloud. "If we could hear them we might find there was less to worry about than we think."

"We'll be limited to pocket equipment," Meester muttered. "And probably have to stay way out of range."

"Consider the possibilities," Jutta suggested. "Tamala leaves the office and our man follows . . ."

"Disaster if he loses him or shows himself," Meester said promptly.

"Somewhere," she continued, "Tamala must meet his comrades and then Smith at the prearranged place. He might have told them where to go or he may lead them there but, one way or another, he will have to bring them together and make identifications. The Comrades will insist on that. We know what Tamala is, and Smith seems to be a fool, but the Russians will be KGB — and not juniors."

She looked for a sign of disagreement but the others just stared back, waiting.

"We don't expect to be able to move in close," she went on. "So the meeting will go ahead in secret unless it is somehow prevented at that point or earlier."

Again she noted the expressions before continuing.

"If the meeting takes place they will probably leave separately and might never come together again. There will be at least three people, possibly four. The Russians will eventually report back to their embassy either directly or indirectly and I would expect Smith to come under KGB surveillance from the time they set eyes on him. Tamala will probably go back to his seedy little office feeling very pleased with himself." The grey lady let both hands fall limply on the table in a gesture of finality. "Well?" she said after a long silence.

De Wet offered her a wan smile. "If only life were so predictable, Jutta."

"So what else?"

"How should I know?"

"You don't think he'll actually hand anything over do you?"

De Wet thought it unlikely. "He wasn't expecting this meeting," he reasoned. "So he hadn't planned to give them anything at this stage. It would put us in a very awkward position if he did. We'd have to have it — one way or another."

Meester scratched his head. "It's hard to see how he can have let them evaluate his offer without giving it away in the first place. What the hell has he still got to bargain with? If he were selling intelligence I could understand it; he gives them a taste and they pay for more. But what kind of intelligence could do what he's claiming for it? We've got to nail him, Frits."

"Sure. But even if we could snatch him from under their noses we might still lose. He's not likely to be on his own in this. If we jump on Mr Smith maybe a Mr Brown somewhere will move even faster on the deal. Our only safe course *was* to find Smith and look him over very carefully before coming out of cover. Now it's too late for that, things have moved too fast for us. We need an entirely new strategy; some way of breaking this crazy puzzle without making it spring the wrong way."

"And not much time for it," Jutta added.

De Wet began toying with a pencil, holding the ends in his fingertips and rotating it like a spindle. "I don't believe we can do it," he said slowly. "Not with our resources and the, er, constraints of protocol here."

It was the reference to protocol that gave the others the drift of his thinking. "You mean hand it over to the Brits?" Meester looked pained.

"I have no better idea. Do you?"

"They'll want a deal," Meester growled, ignoring the question. "They always do. And what do we offer in return this time?"

"Who knows?"

"What's that supposed to mean?"

"Well it depends on what their Great British citizen is trying to sell doesn't it? And who he is. Suppose it is Tyler; from what little we know about him he's not likely to be a senior man in the Ministry of Defence but he might possibly have a job that's connected with a MOD research project. He could certainly have connections of that sort. We are worried because he approached the FAM but in effect he's dealing with the Russians, so I take the view that the British should be as concerned as we are. He's their man, after all."

Meester gave a snort of a laugh. "Maybe we'll get more out of them if we go through the US Embassy; spread the word that they also have a security worry — courtesy of their esteemed NATO ally."

De Wet's expression did not change. "I might do exactly that if I don't get full co-operation. They won't want the Americans involved." It was a point on which they all agreed.

"They could be a lot worse, you know," Jutta reflected. "They often . . ." She hesitated, searching for the right English phrase. "Turn the blind eye to us."

"We are supposed to be on the same side, for Christ's sake. The Boer war is over." Meester looked unconvinced by his own outburst. He liked to tell those who might not know it that the term 'concentration camp' had been coined by Lord Kitchener when Hitler was still a little boy.

Jutta shrugged. "They could be worse."

De Wet looked at her. "They certainly are strange. They make such a thing about privacy and the Englishman's castle and yet British law hardly covers privacy. We can mount a pretty close surveillance operation here and still be perfectly legal."

"I know that, Frits, but we do break a few rules and they choose not to notice."

De Wet spread his hands. "It's understood. We have an agreement. It works both ways."

"Well, that's what I'm saying; there could be no agreement, no understanding."

"And I'm not sure who'd be the losers," Meester muttered.

"We would all lose," de Wet said firmly. "And we'll all lose this one to the Reds if we try to handle it ourselves. Back home there would be no problem but here we suddenly have a situation that we are not prepared for. Whichever way you look at it we need help."

"We'll lose control," Meester grumbled.

"To some extent, yes," de Wet said carefully. "It will be their operation."

Jutta looked at him shrewdly. "But your plan," she murmured.

"Our plan, I hope."

Since the days of the first Queen Elizabeth, British Intelligence has been perfecting the art of secrecy through confusion as well as silence. People are probably better informed now than ever before but few have more than a vague knowledge of how their security is maintained. To be sure, the old wartime Sections 5 and 6 became familiar to everybody as MI5 and MI6 but only long after they had been transformed and the designations reduced to obsolete labels.

The Secret Intelligence Service (MI6) comes under the Foreign and Commonwealth Office. Its chief sits together with the Director General of the Security Service (MI5) on the Joint Intelligence Committee — a Cabinet Subcommittee chaired by the Permanent Under-Secretary of the Foreign Office. In plenary session the JIC would include the Defence Intelligence Staff, the DG of the Government Communications Centre and London representatives of certain allied intelligence services. At this level policies and strategies are agreed upon, intelligence is updated and specialist subcommittees are set up to report on issues which never appear elsewhere in print.

The various branches of British Intelligence have at least one thing in common: they have grown. The total budget for the Security Service is a series of secrets but a lump sum appropriation request, which has to be presented to parliament annually, runs into scores of millions of pounds. This is still tiny by American and Soviet standards. Such a service is not easily accommodated, but the scattering of its many sections throughout London is not entirely a consequence of overspill. To lose a battleship in a city there have to be a lot of separate pieces. Some of them can be made to look like something else. Nor is it easy to manage a service so physically fragmented, but the telephone network is one of the most secure in the world and the staff are uniquely qualified to cope with the sort of problems involved. Each section has a controller with years of service and a very large measure of independence at the operational level. Directives are commonly passed by phone though less familiar equipment may be used to decipher them.

Frits de Wet took a taxi down Whitehall and paid off the driver at the end of King Charles Street. He had no wish to attract attention although there was nothing unusual in a second secretary from the South African Embassy paying a visit to the Foreign and Commonwealth Office. It was, in fact, quite a casual visit. As London-based intelligence officer from a state rated as 'friendly' (though not officially 'allied' within the terms of the JIC) the dour Afrikaner had his allotted contact with British security. It was not a formal arrangement between governments so much as a recognized practice between the two intelligence services. They offered each other a tradesman's entrance for use at the tradesman's level. It did not automatically lead very far but it was a quick way to get attention from higher up. De Wet knew full well that what he was slipping in through the back door should have been cleared by Pretoria and presented with due formality at the front.

His appointment, just within office hours that afternoon, was with one Clive Forest who worked on the Africa desk. What was not generally known, though it was no secret from his close colleagues, was that Forest was a liaison man for the modern MI5. It was an arrangement which filled a special need during state visits and similar occasions when visiting dignitaries insisted on being protected by their own security agents in addition to whatever the British Government was prepared to lay on for them. Collaboration was all well and good but it didn't do to give every foreign friend-of-the-moment a full frontal view of his British counterpart's operations' centre. Instead, he was given an introduction to someone like Clive Forest and a phone number with a guarantee that at any time of day or night his call would be relayed according to his need.

Forest, on the advice of his father, had grown up with the idea of becoming a solicitor and had cultivated, also with his father's encouragement, a calm detachment which had become his natural mien. 'No sense of urgency' some said. 'Absolutely unflappable' others thought. But interpret it as they may, those in terror of Libyan hit squads could detect no more concern in him than those in search of the ground floor toilets. He was in his late forties but his smooth, boyish face made him look younger. He had met de Wet only once since they were first introduced but he could believe that he was not the sort to panic about trifles. If de Wet thought he had an emergency he probably had.

"Hello, Frits." The greeting was casual but not quite offhand; as if they usually caught the same train. "The chap you had last time is on sick leave but I've fixed you up with a more senior man. He should be around somewhere. Have a seat." Forest pressed a button on his intercom and murmured a few words about Mr de Wet from the South African Embassy. The said visitor remained standing with an odd feeling of *déjà vu*. It was almost a verbal replay of his last appointment for a medical check-up.

Forest got to his feet. "We can go straight down," he said.

They went by the stairs although de Wet noticed lift doors at the lower level as they passed. In the corridor there was a sudden bark of laughter from an open doorway, as if somebody had just reached the punch-line of a joke. It died to a chuckling in the throat of a weather-beaten character with a gap in his teeth and a no nonsense haircut. He was holding what looked like a tool bag. A man with an outdoor trade, one might have guessed. In fact Jimmy Baines spent all the time he could on a farm in East Anglia, or fishing wherever he was allowed to, but he often worked indoors and frequently below ground level. After years in the diplomatic wireless service the Norfolk-born farmer's son was familiar with the secret communications equipment of half the British embassies in the world. He was also an expert on short-range electronic devices that were now so small that their thread-like antennae could be embedded in wallpaper. The bucolic Mr Baines, now retired from world travel, was one of London's most trusted 'office sweepers'. If anybody knew the layout of British security at home, he did. But then human beings don't come more secure than Jimmy Baines. And in any case, it had often been remarked, no bloody foreigner would ever understand him.

Still grinning, Jimmy ambled away as Forest approached, and a slightly bewildered de Wet was delivered to the man who remained at the open door. There was an exchange of Christian names, a brief handshake and Forest withdrew.

They talked in a small annexe to a large, empty conference room. There were soft chairs and a glass-topped table but otherwise the room was conspicuously bare. "Can't offer you a drink here I'm afraid but at short notice it seemed the best place to bring you."

De Wet dismissed the regrets with a little wave and said

"excellent". He saw an older, smaller man, lightly built with pure white hair and piercing blue eyes. He was tastefully though not expensively dressed in a dark suit with a plain tie. He could rightfully have worn any one of several ties testifying to a highly academic background — but he did not possess them. Leaning back he steepled his fingers and regarded de Wet steadily, waiting for him to begin.

In the streets above, the afternoon rush was in full cry. It was a phenomenon unmistakable even in satellite photographs. The bustling millions of a vibrant city were joined in the common purpose of going home. Human streams converged and slowed and swelled in a thousand places while underground trains hurtled past stations which looked like the players' view from the touch-line. Seven miles from King Charles Street, and north by a hundred thousand souls, a very pale, red haired man was already home, for he had not left his tiny flat all day. At the sink a half-eaten meal crusted a cheap plate and empty cans stood on the draining-board. The single bed was not made but the counterpane was pulled over and he lay upon it, fully dressed. His hands were clasped behind his head and his eyes were closed. From time to time he would take a deep breath very slowly. Keith Tyler was not ill but he was trying to suppress the mounting tension which made it so hard to concentrate. He was anxious to be mentally prepared for his appointment the following afternoon. It worried him a great deal.

FIVE

JAMES RANDOLPH DID not go home at all. His meeting with de Wet lasted for more than two hours, and after that he returned alone to his own headquarters where he spent the best part of another two hours on the telephone. He made five calls in all, two of them very brief and one of them extremely lengthy. After that he sat and ate sandwiches which he had collected on his way back from the Foreign Office. By that time it was dark outside but it made no difference for in Randolph's office there were no windows. The space was ample but there was no attempt to disguise the fact that he worked from a basement room which had originally been intended as a store for the huge office-block above. Eland House (together with a large annexe) accommodates the Overseas Development Administration and Randolph considered himself lucky to be located there. It was only a few minutes from Victoria Station whereas some units, he knew, had to operate from cramped quarters in far less convenient parts of the city.

Leading off the main office were two smaller rooms, one of them containing toilets, a shower cubicle and the rudiments of a kitchen. There was also an outer office where an elderly lady performed the usual secretarial routine although most of the files were stored in a specially fortified bank of cabinets let into the wall of the inner sanctum. Randolph searched through them for some time and at one point he tapped out a few words on a computer terminal but seemed disappointed by the results. He also took two incoming calls which sounded less than exciting.

A little before midnight he selected the best of three folding camp-beds from a cupboard and looked over his little cache of clean linen: it wasn't worth going home to the south suburbs for a few hours' sleep. There had been a time when he would have checked into a decent hotel, but there was always a fuss about reimbursement and on nights as late as this all he really wanted was somewhere to lie down.

He was awake at six and ready to receive visitors by seven — not that there was any need to prepare for the one who arrived at that hour. He let himself in, hung up his hat and coat and made straight for the teapot. Randolph was already on the telephone and he raised a hand in silent greeting. He and Bill Fletcher had worked together for eleven years.

"Have we got another flap on, James, or is this all your idea?" He placed his cup very carefully on the desk and allowed his stocky body to slump into a chair.

After the call Randolph jotted a few more words on his sheet before looking up. "It's an odd one, this, Bill. Nobody is panicking yet because no one knows what to make of it but de Wet's little team has rather put us on the spot. He's being cagey about his sources but de Wet claims that a British national is about to finalize a deal with the Free Africa Movement and Russia has agreed to pay for it."

Fletcher raised his eyebrows but there was otherwise little change in his heavy features. He began to search his pockets for tobacco, pipe and matches but found he'd left them in his coat. "He'll have to tell us a lot more than that," he replied as he heaved himself to his feet. He was in his fifties but had always moved as though he weighed twice as much as he did.

"I think he told us most of what he knows and it was enough to convince me that we can't afford to ignore it. A man with an English accent approached the Free Africa Movement here with an offer of something that he claimed would give them — and I quote — an advantage that could tip the balance for them. He was speaking in a military context." He held up a hand to forestall Fletcher's question. "I'll show you the transcript in a minute, Bill. I know what you are thinking but there's a factor which lifts this out of that category. You see, de Wet believes, and on the evidence I agree with him, that the FAM had this offer evaluated by their Russian friends and the Russians themselves have asked to meet this enterprising countryman of ours."

Fletcher paused at the point of striking a match. "Christ. I hope he's not from Porton Down."

"Precisely. They have a description of sorts and he looks something like this." Randolph reached across with the photograph.

Fletcher frowned at it and slowly shook his head.

"No, nothing on him at all," Randolph agreed. "They have quite a full dossier: name, date of birth, passport number and so on. His name is Tyler and he lived in South Africa for two years so their people had him on file. Of course it may not be the right man."

"Well does it seem likely? I mean what does this chap do?"

Randolph's sharp blue eyes seemed to be focussed somewhere in mid air and he spoke as if to himself when he said, "The term chemist covers an awful lot of ground doesn't it? Over there he worked for a firm called Pharmatech. Laboratory job. Involved with pharmaceuticals."

"Drugs? Narcotics?"

"Possibly. I don't know, Bill. One can think of so many possibilities." And he seemed to be doing just that.

"Where is he now?"

"Ah, yes. That's the point you see. They haven't been able to find him and there's reason to think that his audience with the Comrades might be this afternoon. The South Africans are relying on Gabriel Tamala to show us the way."

Fletcher started up his pipe in silence. Over the years unnecessary explanation had become offensive to them both. It was felt, without consciously considering it, to be an insult to the other's intellect.

"He's not likely to be alone, our countryman."

"No."

"And if it's only a watch and see job they'd do it themselves."

"Quite. They want it nipped in the bud."

"Jumped on from a great height if I know them. I can see the problem though."

"De Wet had a rather exotic analogy. He said it was like seeing a mamba crawling into the cot with the baby. It has to be stopped but when all you can see to grab is a bit in the middle it's a very risky business."

"And did he have any bright ideas?"

"He came up with the germ of a plan, yes. A two phase approach. That's why you're here now, Bill. We agreed on a procedure and to start with, at least, the South Africans will keep out of it. Special Branch are taking over and I've promised to keep de Wet informed."

"Tell me; is de Wet keeping his own people informed?"

Randolph passed a hand over his snow-white hair. "I suspect not. There would have been a different approach otherwise."

"That's what I thought. It's all a bit unlikely isn't it? Quite honestly I'm surprised you've got the green light to make this an SB operation. I take it you *have*, James."

"Oh yes. There's strong evidence that a Briton is secretly trying to sell some military advantage to the Russians. We must respond to that. Any South African involvement is purely incidental."

"It won't be if they upset Gabriel Tamala. He'll go straight to Fleet Street. London Representative of Free Africa Movement harrassed by police." He closed his eyes and managed a grimace.

"Everything to do with South Africa is a diplomatic minefield, Bill. The only people who have all the answers are those who haven't heard all the questions. Anyway, the diplomats are not in on this one, you are. I've arranged for you to brief the SB team as soon as we are finished here. Daintry is expecting you."

The girl in the phone box looked up but had no intention of cutting short her call just because somebody was hovering a couple of feet from her elbow. She produced what she hoped was a withering look and turned her back. "You get some cheeky sods, don't you," she continued conversationally. "There's one outside nearly trying to get in. If he's got an emergency he can say so; otherwise he can wait his turn." Just as she hoped, the red-haired man could hear her plainly and was not prepared to make an issue of it. Even at a public phone booth he felt tense. When she eventually left, without a glance in his direction, he slipped inside with a coin ready in his fingers, and dialled a local number.

"Smith," he said huskily. "I've talked it over with those I represent and we agree. I'm on my way now but tell your friends I'm not prepared to play games. Any clever tricks; any sort of nonsense, and it's off. On my way then, okay?"

Tamala assured him that they would simply meet as planned.

In South Africa House Chris Collins collected the longest recording of Smith's voice that he had made and he wished he could tell Sue how exciting his job had suddenly become. De Wet actually smiled when he heard the tapes. To have the meeting confirmed on the day was the sort of windfall he had learned not to expect. He dialled a number that he had been given and passed the news that the Special Branch team would not be wasting their time.

Up to ten per cent of Britain's police are employed in the Criminal Investigation Department — the CID. A hundred years ago an offshoot of the CID was formed into a Special Irish Branch to deal with republican terrorists. Nowadays the Special Branch handles a lot more than the problems of Ireland, but then a hundred years is a long time in which to gain experience and it spans an evolutionary era in technology. In the streets of London the men and women of the SB do their specializing on home ground. In teams, or as loners, they represent the state-of-the-art in covert operations with a political element. In partnership with agents of the security service they work to mutual benefit but only the SB has police powers.

Commander Daintry had no fondness for short-notice jobs, but fielding a team of five for a few quiet hours in N1 was the sort of nuisance he could take with his tea and biscuits. Not that he underestimated the calibre of the officers required: they'd have to be good if professionals from the other side were involved. Bill Fletcher laboured that point during his briefing, but by that time the officers had already been selected and kitted out. By noon they were in position.

Keith Tyler forced himself to wait until nearly half-past two before leaving the saloon bar of the Crown and starting his walk to the rendezvous. He had drunk nearly nothing and felt no need for it. He was far from relaxed but had managed to work up such a strength of resolve that he was actually fuelled by determination. You can do it, he told himself repeatedly. Cool, that's what you need in this life, the nerve to take the big chance when it comes. They all told the same story when they got to the top: I was

63

lucky . . . right place at the right time . . . gamble paid off . . . never looked back. Well, if luck had any part in it, it still had to be given a chance. Nothing venture nothing win. In the end it came back to the same thing: nerve.

He saw Tamala first, standing reading a newspaper near the entrance to the tube. Same overcoat and silly hat. Sunglasses too. He appeared to be alone and for an instant Tyler felt a pang of something like disappointment. He was mentally screwed-up in preparation for this meeting. He would stand firm no matter what pressure they tried to exert. But a loss of interest by the other party was the one thing, he suddenly realized, for which he was not prepared. Tactics, he assured himself. They won't *want* to seem keen. It's the most elementary rule of doing business from the street corner to the board room. Tamala had seen him now. Obvious recognition but no greeting. He had checked his watch and started towards the ticket barrier, sorting coins in the palm of his hand. Tyler moved abreast of him and he looked up in feigned surprise.

"So we meet again, Mr Smith."

"I always knew we would, Mr Tamala. Where are your friends?"

"They will be here. We must be careful you know."

"Of course." Tyler felt a surge of excitement and a return of his confidence. They passed through the barriers and rode the escalator a few steps apart. Tamala unhesitatingly followed the sign for the Circle line and lingered a moment at the platform until Tyler once again came abreast.

"Near the other end I think," Tamala said.

It was a quiet time of day for the underground; a trickle before the flood. People stood silently, facing the lines and the advertisements which on the far side, were out of reach and undefiled by felt pens. A knot of youngsters giggled and fooled under the 'Way Out' sign. One of them stepped back to act out his story with mime. Three or four individuals paced solemnly back and forth in their chosen sectors, studiously avoiding each other and the lanky redhead who was in desultory conversation with a black man. Tyler kept close to the wall as they sauntered to the very end of the platform.

The man who approached them, casually, was a broad shouldered figure of about fifty. He was hatless and bald. He kept his hands in the pockets of his short overcoat but greeted them in what struck

Tyler as a satirical tone, as if he were mocking their own cloak and dagger behaviour. Tyler looked at him keenly but saw only broad, open features. What had he expected? Furtive characters in fur hats?

"Not the best place to talk business, Mr Smith," the stranger said in accentless English. "But it has its advantages." He turned to face the length of the platform, his dark eyes flickering over the waiting passengers as if he were expecting someone else to join them. "And this should not take very long," he went on. "We have looked at your product and we agree that it could possibly have some value to our friend's cause." He indicated Tamala by a stiff little gesture that resembled as incipient bow. It struck Tyler as being distinctly un-English.

"Good. Well I don't see that there is much more to discuss. I've stated our terms so if the sample was satisfactory . . ."

"Oh, things are never so simple, you know that," the other said expansively.

"It's pretty straightforward as far as I'm concerned." Tyler retorted.

"There *are* things to consider," Tamala purred. "Half a million pounds is a lot of money."

"Half the price of a decent helicopter," Tyler said promptly. "A lot to you and me but peanuts to those who say they support you. How much military hardware gets wrecked in similar causes? It has to be reckoned in billions."

"That is not the point, Mr Smith." The soothing tone again carried a trace of mockery but there was no humour in the man's face; no clue at all to his feelings. He remained only alert and watchful. "You surely want some security before you arrange any deliveries?"

"Naturally."

"Well then. We also need to be certain before any payments can be made. These are the sort of details we have to discuss. I am sure you have thought about it. Now we must put our thoughts together." His last words were lost in the din of an approaching train. The display panel said CIRCLE and it stopped, collecting more passengers than it put down. But a few of those who had been waiting remained on the platform, needing a train on the

65

Metropolitan line. Only a few were at that end of the platform. There was a girl with an art folder and an older couple leaning back against the wall, holding hands. A man in overalls was still pacing. The art student alone remained conspicuous among a spate of newcomers some of whom were hurrying, too late, as the train pulled away.

Tyler was the first to speak as the booming echo died in the tunnel. "I don't see much security problem from your point of view. I have an account with a Zurich Bank and as soon as you deposit the money I'll produce the stuff. You can keep me on a short lead until you're satisfied with it."

Tamala appeared to be considering this in some depth but the other merely inclined his bald head and said, "Of course we can make some such arrangement when the time comes."

"So what's the problem?" Tyler demanded.

"No problem at all. But we don't see any great urgency. In fact we would like to test another sample."

It seemed to Tyler that Tamala was taken aback by this but he recovered himself quickly. Tyler stared at them both with frank suspicion. "What the hell is this? You've done all that and if you were not impressed you wouldn't be here."

Broad shoulders lifted in a trace of a shrug. "I am not a technical man. I can only tell you what I know. Another sample is needed for testing. The last one was, I believe, in some way, er, destabilized."

"Well of course it was. You don't expect to be given pure strain viable material as a sample do you? That's what I'm offering for sale: a culture that you can use for further production."

"As I say, I am not a technical man."

Tyler glared at Tamala who looked away. He appeared to have had his own instructions to keep his mouth shut and not get involved. The tunnel filled with noise again and Tyler tried hard to think while they observed the change of faces for the second time. When the train pulled away there were only four people left on the platform. None of them, Tyler thought, had been there when he first arrived. He turned to look squarely at the one he had to deal with.

"All right," he said evenly. "I'll get you another sample. And you can show good faith by coming up with ten percent — in cash. What do you say?"

Newcomers were now appearing in quick succession and the man's eyes did not leave the entrance gates as he replied. "Fifty thousand pounds." It sounded like a statement. "And I suppose you would like it in small used notes."

"Preferably. Why not?" Tyler said flatly. *Was* he being mocked?

"From your side I can think of no reason at all. How are we to keep contact?"

"The same way we have been doing: I call Mr Tamala."

"I hope you are careful what you say over the phone, Mr Smith."

"Naturally."

Tamala just nodded.

"Well, let's leave it at that for now. I will pass on what you say and tell you the reaction through our friend here. Give me three days from today; I should have something by then." He offered a hand and Tyler shook it, uncertainly. When he then turned to Tamala the handshake was firm and if the African was disappointed by the outcome of the brief meeting he did not show it. They walked away and left Tyler standing there, at the end of the platform.

He stayed there for several minutes, struggling to collect his thoughts. It hadn't been quite what he expected but he was not too discouraged; the project was still on. Disturbing afterthoughts as to what he should or should not have said just had to be borne. He was used to them anyway; they shadowed his every conversation. Socially awkward though he was, Keith Tyler was not naive. He expected to be followed. It was inconceivable that Tamala and his friends would not want to know more about him but they had asked no questions — knowing that he would give nothing away. Now they would have him followed to find out where he lived, who he was and how he came to possess such a secret. He stared suspiciously at the line-out along the platform but there was nothing to be learned by looking. He found the ticket with which he had come through the barrier. Why not use it? If they were trying to follow him they'd have to be prepared for every possibility but why make it easy for them by going straight out on to the street? He waited for the next train and then waited until the last moment before springing aboard. He tried to see if anybody else was doing the same thing but he hadn't a clear view. People were standing too close to the train.

The carriage was half empty and no one paid him the slightest attention. At Great Portland Street he got out, walked towards the exit and then slipped back into another carriage. At Baker Street he changed platforms and caught a southbound train on the Bakerloo line. At Regent's Park he stepped on to the platform, looked both ways and then quickly stepped back, knocking into a woman with a shopping bag. "Make up your mind," she chided and Tyler felt a fool. At Oxford Circus he changed to the Central line and completed the third leg of a square by taking an eastbound train to Tottenham Court Road. There he strode briskly towards the escalator which led to the street.

Tyler's gangling build and bright red hair made him an easy figure to follow and for that Daintry's little team was truly thankful. By the time he had reached Baker Street they had spotted the tail that he had rightly suspected would be attached to him. By Tottenham Court Road they were satisfied that the tail was alone. Tyler, by that time, had just about concluded that if anybody had started out behind him they were not there now. He reached the escalator and carried on walking, his long legs carrying him swiftly past those who were standing obediently on the right. He got off at the top with scarcely a break in his stride and did not look back. He did not see the woman stumble and fall behind him. There was a cry and he sensed some commotion but when he turned he saw only that people were milling at the head of the escalator. There was a glimpse of a bright red dress at floor level and he realized that a woman must have fallen, but by then he was on his way out. He was not sure whether the emergency stop had been used on the moving stairway and it certainly never occurred to him that the woman could have been the one with the shopping bag that he had barged into at Regent's Park. If he had tried to recall he would have said that she was wearing some drab coloured coat.

The woman (whose coat was folded over her arm — and shopping bag) was able to delay the KGB for only a few precious seconds. In that time her partner, on the adjacent fixed stair, had to by-pass the floor show and position himself immediately behind Tyler. This he did just as Tyler reached the ticket control and found he had extra to pay. He slapped some coins in front of the ticket collector instead of going over to the separate window. The collector yelled at him but Tyler hurried on even faster. This worked to the advantage of Daintry's man because Tyler's turn of speed took him round the corner an instant before the mêlée on the escalator had been sorted out. He was safely out of sight therefore when he felt his elbow seized in a powerful grip and found himself being steered neatly into a draper's shop. His protests died in his throat at the sight of the Special Branch identification.

"Daintry sounds very pleased. Says if it had been a training run he'd have given them nine out of ten." Bill Fletcher fished about in an old briefcase as he plodded over to his desk. He produced a brown paper envelope and a miniature tape cassette which he handed to James Randolph. "These are copies. He hasn't wasted any time I must say."

"Where's Tyler now?" Randolph asked as he opened the envelope.

"Still at Albany Street. They're letting him sweat for a bit but Daintry wants to confer with us as soon as possible on the interrogation. In the meantime they'll do all the personal details routine."

"Does he know what he's being held on?"

"Oh, yes. Prevention of terrorism. He knows he can be held on suspicion for a week under that little act. Apparently he's playing the innocent."

Randolph slid out the photographs and spread them on the desk. "These are extremely good," he murmured, holding one at arm's length. All three subjects were facing the camera as they stood looking down the length of the underground platform. "Gabriel Tamala looks a bit subdued. I don't recognize his friend at all do you?"

Fletcher shook his head. "Neither did Daintry but one of his chaps stayed with him after he and Tamala left the tube. They'll put something together on him in due course. That will be a bonus for us but I don't doubt he's KGB."

"Who else could he be?" Randolph was scrutinizing another picture. "At least Tyler should have been easy enough to keep in sight; he appears to be about six foot two."

69

"Just as well he is, James. I gather he gave them quite a runaround."

Randolph replaced the photographs and picked up the cassette. "Have you heard this?"

"Not yet. Just brought it straight round." Together they walked into the side room where projectors, recorders and other electronic gadgetry were kept. They listened to the tape without speaking though their thoughts were clear enough in the faces they made. It was a faint recording and at times the voices were inaudible or the words indistinct but the gist of the conversation was fairly clear.

"They did well to get anything at all in the circumstances," Randolph remarked as he rewound the reel.

"Clever stuff," Fletcher agreed. "Daintry told me about it. They couldn't use a directional mike but they had a sort of dish antenna thing like a two-foot saucer," he floated his hands in a curve. "Must have been pretty slim because one of them had it in an art folio. Same one took the pictures, he said."

Randolph shook his head. "The technical people left me behind years ago."

Fletcher worked at his pipe while they heard the tape for a second time. "Nervous, I'd say. Our friend Tyler."

Randolph nodded. "He has cause to be."

"Daintry said he'll keep us informed as the personal stuff comes out. I think he meant don't call us, we'll call you. What about de Wet?"

Randolph looked slightly troubled. "De Wet. Yes indeed, what about de Wet. I've told him he was right about Tyler and that he's been picked up. They are very keen to get at him."

"With a blunt instrument, no doubt."

"That's what bothers me. Frits de Wet's no fool, as I've said before, but I'd like to handle our man very carefully from now on. I'm afraid it could be disastrous if we let the South Africans in. It's a question of choosing one's words, Bill."

Fletcher nodded emphatically. "You don't have to tell me. We'll just have to hold them off." He suddenly grinned over his pipe. "Well, there's not much they can do about it is there?"

Randolph still looked uneasy. "We agreed that the pick-up

should be left to Special Branch but it was understood that we would collaborate with de Wet after that."

Fletcher shrugged. "There's still not much they can do about it."

It is questionable whether leaving Tyler to sweat for a bit was a good thing or not. At the time of his arrest, and subsequent removal from the back of the draper's shop in an unmarked car, he was shocked almost speechless. When he heard that he was being detained for questioning under the Prevention of Terrorism Act he could scarcely believe it, but he was still sufficiently in control of his wits to realize that the less he said the better. He wanted time to think and the hours he spent alone in the police station cell were not wasted. The police had his name and a few personal history details. No doubt they would follow up with a thorough investigation, but where would it get them? If Tamala talked they would have part of the story but no evidence. Only one person, other than himself, could provide them with all they needed and they still had no direct link to that person. That they should find such a link was Tyler's greatest fear as he sat bow-backed in his cell with his head in his hands.

But behind Tyler's fear there was a stubbornness from which he drew strength as the hours passed. Don't lose your nerve, he warned himself again and again. Only the frightened, the flustered and the fools tell them what they want. Settle on a story and stick to it. If they ask different questions give them the same old answers — a thousand times over if need be. They might get the secret from somebody but they'll never get it from you. Stay cool. Defy them.

And it was a very defiant suspect indeed that they came to question when they thought the time was ripe.

SIX

WHILE KEITH TYLER was mentally preparing himself for his inquisition the person who was uppermost in his mind was struggling to keep his thoughts on his job. Fifty miles away, on the western outskirts of Cambridge, Doctor Ralph Conway checked his figures for the third time and entered a note in what looked like a heavy desk diary. He was slightly younger than Tyler, much shorter, and lightly built to the point of being girlish. Deft fingers turned the tap of a burette and small, neat features were held as if for a photograph as he watched the liquid run into a flask. He had performed the same titration only an hour before but had forgotten to record the result. It was the sort of chore that he would normally have given to an assistant but he needed something to look busy with; some pottering job until he could get back to more demanding work.

He glanced at the clock for the hundredth time. Another half hour to keep up the show of being busy. Above the partition he could see Jolliffe's dome of a head bowed over the desk. Nit-picking his way through the reports, no doubt. *As unit co-ordinator I have to answer to the directors, you know*. Yes, headmaster. Conway realized he was biting his lip again. The library would be easier to bear for the last half hour. He stood up and removed his white lab coat then packed his calculator and some loose sheets in a slim briefcase. Quietly he walked out, letting the glass-panelled door swing softly back on its pneumatic levers. The air conditioners hummed a different note as he turned the corner that led to the Central Research Library. Another softly sighing door opened into a spacious room with wide, polished tables, comfortable chairs and fixed, rectangular reading-lamps. Walls of shelving were arranged geometrically and packed solid with books, box files and volumes of abstruse journals that looked like blocks of printer's stock. There were about half a dozen people there and the only sound was the whirr and click of a photocopier. Conway selected a treatise on 'Some Aspects of Prophage Induction' but settled down to worry about entirely different things.

Through the window he could see across the spring-green turf to the mahonia shrubbery which bordered the section where he worked. At first the job had seemed like a continuation of his university days: the same sort of environment with its clean new brickwork and well kept grounds, the familiar laboratory régime. As a student there had been the worry of getting a good degree followed by the anxiety of a research project which turned out to have been ill-chosen. Always there had been stress but in retrospect they had been carefree days compared with the present. At five o'clock Conway went back to his lab and was seen to be putting his bench notes in order before going home. Research staff were not required to punch time-cards but Jolliffe noticed things like punctuality.

He made his way to the block exit and joined a loose throng heading for the car park. He drove his Renault on to the perimeter road which followed the high chain-link fence towards the main gates. The new vaccine complex had cost millions and a significant proportion of it had gone into satisfying the council and other authorities that the place would be secure. The plant had recycled water, air purification, low pressure chambers, high temperature incineration and was surrounded by a security fence. But things were only as secure as the people who worked them.

It was about a quarter of an hour's drive to get home. The countryside was uninspiring, open and monotonous without grandeur; rich and green without charm. He drew up at an old gabled house with an iron gate and a neglected garden to the side. On the other side was a paved square with a roughly constructed car port. He left the Renault there and walked slowly to the heavy front door.

The village was tiny, though a plan for a new housing development of some two dozen units was proclaimed by a builder's sign. It would be, inevitably, another dormitory for Cambridge. Ketley had never been more than a hamlet although it was smaller now than in former days. At one time the community had at least supported a one-class primary school but now the few village kids went by bus to a comprehensive four miles away and Ralph Conway lived in the old school house. He was no closer to Nettiscombe than if he had lived in the city but accommodation in Cambridge would have cost him twice as much. Besides, the old house had suited him perfectly. There he could be himself and do what he found interesting in life. He interfered with nobody and the handful of villagers were content to leave him alone once they had satisfied their curiosity about him.

For a time, after the school had closed, the house had stood empty and the adjacent classroom had been used for Women's Institute meetings and occasional village functions. It was the WI which had pressed the education authority to do something with the house before the damp or the squatters got in. It was decided to sell it but there had been a foul-up over the auction announcement and only four people turned up. The reserve price wasn't reached and Conway bought it with an offer the very next day. It had more space than he needed even after he had turned the main bedroom into a private laboratory.

He made coffee, switched on the TV and flipped it off again, turning instead to a newspaper. After a few minutes he tossed that aside and sat back with his head at rest and his eyes closed but he could not relax. At Nettiscombe he struggled to maintain appearances and hold down a job. At home he abandoned himself to worry and to the nightmare that had come to dominate his waking life.

It was more than a year since it had happened and in some ways it was easier now; panic can only be acute, never chronic. He had not known Tyler long at that time. They had met at a British Association meeting. Keith had approached him during the conversazione to discuss a paper that Conway had just presented. For reasons that Conway still found indefinable and disturbing they had struck up an immediate friendship.

"So where are you staying now?"

"Well I thought I'd go back tonight. I've been living with mother in Stoke since I returned to England. Just until I get myself fixed up, you know."

"Stoke! But that's miles. You'll be travelling half the night. Look, come and stay with me. There's plenty of room and you can leave in the morning."

Tyler hadn't hesitated. "That's very good of you. Thanks."

Nothing had happened between them that night, nor on any of Keith's subsequent visits but he knew that there could be more than just friendship if they allowed it to be so. Like a man with his neighbour's wife Conway had tried to take pride in his own self-denial but he needed constant reassurance that he was not also deluding himself. Small things were enough: a look, a word, a touch. Nobody at Nettiscombe knew about Keith any more than they knew about the home laboratory.

He had confided in Keith because he was not involved. Keith could understand a friend's consuming interest in pure research. He could accept it without wanting details. He could see that it was the main thing in his friend's life. Indeed, there had been little else to life, but Conway would have given anything for a return to that happy state. Now he knew no peace at all.

The nightmare had begun on the last Saturday in March of the previous year. Keith had telephoned to say that his car was laid up and he would be arriving by train. Conway had shopping and other things to do in Cambridge, so he spent most of the day in the town, driving to the station at 7 p.m. to meet Tyler's train.

On the platform they shook hands and embraced briefly, searching each other's eyes as they drew apart. "I'm glad you could come. What happened to the car?"

"Oh, I don't know. It's juddering like a road drill. Clutch, I think. Nothing I can put right anyway."

They walked over to the Renault, Tyler pivoting his old suitcase against his knee while Conway fished for the key. He drove slowly through the town and out on to the A45 to cruise steadily westwards.

"Any luck with the job hunt yet?"

"No, not really. Nothing I'm prepared to consider anyway. I'm getting pretty sick of being told how many honours graduates are on the dole. It's the standard phraseology for saying that with a diploma you aren't in the running." He peered forward as they approached a small shape on the road. "What was that?"

"Dead hare I think. They are still quite common round here. They seem to like it flat."

"Well that one's flat enough," Tyler quipped. "Mad as a March hare. Or jugged hare. Now there's a dish. You stew it with wine . . ." And Conway let him change the subject.

By the time they reached the Sandy turning the night air was chilling and the headlights from the car were swathed in a gentle white mist. There were few other cars on that stretch of the journey but Conway kept to the same steady, even cautious, speed. Twice they passed the cheery lights of a village pub and for short distances there were street lamps and sprays of shining mist. Then the darkness of the lanes again with its softly looming shapes.

"It was really quite bad along here a couple of months ago. This stuff freezes on the road and when you hit a smooth patch you can end up in the ditch."

"I can imagine. We're nearly there now aren't we?"

"Two or three minutes. The turning's just up on the right." Conway eased his foot on the pedal and stared expectantly at the far verge, then he swung over and the flashing orange light seemed to surround them. Two cottage windows appeared as an obscure glow between the trees. A little bus shelter came into view with a post but no sign on top. A single street lamp towered above a tiny green, and beyond it there were a few more lights but neither sight nor sound of activity in the village. Ketley had never had a pub; Kingsbourne, only two miles away, had two.

"Well, here we are then." Conway began brightly. And then he stopped and frowned. "Who on earth is this?"

A dark coloured Ford Capri was parked on the hard standing next to Conway's car port.

"Don't you know the car?" Tyler craned for a better view.

"I don't think so." Conway was still frowning as he parked the Renault and they climbed out. Subconsciously, affected perhaps by the mist or the eerie silence and the little mystery before them, they both closed their door quietly. "Unless it's Chandler's. He drives a Capri. But what would he be doing here?"

"Who's Chandler?"

"He works in our unit."

"Probably a friendly visit then."

Conway did not reply. He produced his door key and went ahead without another word. Tyler followed.

★

76

Barry Chandler was sitting comfortably in Conway's lounge with a glass of whisky. He was a big, smoothly handsome man with slicked hair and an arrogant self-assurance that Conway detested. He was in his thirties but might have been older. He held a job in research administration for which, in Conway's opinion, he was not qualified. But what Chandler lacked in intellect he could make up for in charm and manner when it suited his purpose. Conway had earned his successes and it seemed to him that Chandler and others like him had got where they were by talking and posturing.

"What are you doing here?" Spots of colour burned on the scientist's cheeks.

"Waiting for you, *doctor* Conway."

"But how did you get in?"

"Oh, you left the door open." He produced a sweet smile of insincerity. "I dropped by to return this book of yours but then I found it so interesting here I decided to wait for you."

Conway glared at the book. It was a textbook which Chandler had borrowed from his bench at the lab. It gave some excuse, the thinnest possible for a visit, he supposed. But Chandler felt he needed no excuse and the smug, gloating look on his face was a clear signal of the fact.

"That's rubbish, Barry. And you didn't find the door open either. Now what are you doing here?"

"Aren't you going to introduce me to your rangy friend?"

Conway turned and saw that Tyler was watching them impassively. "No, I'm not. To be quite honest we don't want your company so if you can't say what you want then I'd be glad if you'd leave." As he spoke Conway strutted to the door and held it ajar.

Chandler smiled for effect again. "Oh, do stop the drama, Ralph. You've been caught being naughty so just sit down and tell me all about it."

For a moment Conway was confused by the rather camp choice of words. Was Chandler really suggesting . . . ? No, that was impossible. He had no grounds, nobody had. But did he suspect it?

Chandler must have sensed that Conway's uncertainty was real because his next words were blunt and explicit.

"Look. I said cut out the crap. You've got a whole bloody

Nettiscombe subsidiary up there and I want to know about it. All about it, right?"

So that was it. He'd been snooping round the house and had found the lab. Conway stiffened with sudden fury.

"Why, you slimy swine. You come here, force your way in, poke and pry around my home and then calmly demand an explanation from *me*. You should be doing all the explaining, not me." He swung round to face Tyler, automatically seeking support. Tyler looked more surprised than anything else but he nodded agreement without taking his eyes off Chandler.

Chandler was unmoved. He passed a hand slowly over his hair and sighed as if he were weary of explaining the obvious. "When you've got over your tantrums, Ralph, just try to think will you? We are all expected to do our bit in protecting the firm's interests so when I see you stealing valuable equipment I take notice."

"Stealing! There's no question of stealing. I'm just using some stuff at home that's all. It will go back when I've . . ."

"That's what everybody says when they get caught. I just borrowed it, I meant to give it back. Well, as I say, I take notice. So when I come round here and find your door open I come in, calling out, nothing slimy as you call it. And then . . ."

"The door was locked and you damned well know it."

"You can say that. You might even think that but I say you're mistaken. I also say that what you are doing with the firm's equipment is in clear breach of the safety and security regulations, of great concern to the health authorities and no doubt will fascinate the drug squad."

At that Conway let out a bitter snort of a laugh.

"That's idiotic. You wouldn't know drugs from toffee, you stupid, meddling fool. You haven't a clue when it comes to serious work. You can only think in terms of money. You see a refining process upstairs and you think it has to be narcotics. Oh, Conway's making millions on the side; I'll have a share of that. Is that what you thought? Is that why you're here?"

Chandler's eyes narrowed and he coloured slightly but his sense of theatre was instinctive and when he spoke he did so quietly and deliberately in contrast to Conway's outburst. "All right, *doctor*

Conway. If I'm so wrong then put me right. Explain it to me. Do as I say and tell me all about it."

"You wouldn't understand," Conway said contemptuously. "You couldn't."

Chandler stood up then. He was still holding the whisky glass and he put it down with exaggerated calm. His hand was steady. "Very well. Let's see if the board will be any more understanding, shall we? And don't think about rushing to put everything back where it came from because I have a feeling that you won't be allowed on the premises until this little lot has been investigated. Of course, you could bury it all in the garden and deny everything but then you couldn't explain the evidence I've got could you."

Conway was now struggling for control. The muscles of his face were fixed in a rigid sneer so that he looked like a child trying not to cry. "Just tell me what you want and then get out."

Chandler stopped half-way to the door. "But I can't tell you anything until you've explained things to me. Isn't that right?"

"It's not what you think, that's the point." The scientist closed his eyes and shook his head emphatically. "It really is research. I'm interested in invasion mechanisms in viruses. I've been working on bacteriophages mostly and it probably won't lead to anything at all. I'm just finding out what I can, that's all."

"Are you telling me that you have no clear objectives? That you spend hours beavering away up there just for the fun of it?"

"Well that's how it is with pure research. It's only when you've got the facts that you can think about applications."

"Then why aren't you doing this openly at work?"

"I should have thought that was perfectly obvious," Conway choked. "At work we're commercial aren't we? The firm decides what it wants and we try to produce it. They want profits. They aren't keen on having staff following their fancies."

"Or modifying processes to avoid patents. Or serving up little offerings to rival companies. You're not being very convincing I'm afraid. But I'll seek a second opinion." And with that Chandler turned purposefully towards the door.

"No, wait! Keith, stop him." There was an urgency in Conway's voice that brought an instant response from his friend. Tyler stepped in front of the door. Chandler's lips tightened and he hunched his shoulders, barging Tyler aside while he reached for the door handle with his left hand. It was a mistake, but then Chandler did not know Keith Tyler. He was extremely intolerant of being pushed around and though he lacked beef there was surprising strength in his stringy body. He spun in a half turn and caught Chandler with a wild, flailing kidney punch. It drew a gasp of pain and Chandler lunged forward intending to knock Tyler well clear. Tyler was faster and jabbed a bony fist hard into the other's face. It drew blood but failed to stop the charge. The two collided in a moment of violent temper. Chandler was still trying to push Tyler away so that he could leave but it was not that easy. The gawky Tyler was clutching and grappling like a predatory bird and he brought both of them sprawling to the floor. Chandler had the advantage and from a half standing position he knocked Tyler flat with a single, savage blow. Panting, he glared at Conway and made again for the door.

There is no doubt that Tyler wanted to stop Chandler from leaving but it was blind rage more than any purpose that pushed him to his feet and sent him leaping at the man's back. Conway had been using a hammer to tack down a curling carpet edge. Tyler, much later, said that he could not remember how he came to have it in his hand but he brought it down with terrible force at the base of Chandler's skull. Then he flung the hammer aside and grabbed Chandler by the shoulders, pulling him back and swinging him away from the door. Chandler tottered a few steps, his arm jerking as if he were still clawing for the handle. He fell like a massive rag doll, smashing a low coffee table beneath him.

For several seconds the only sound was Tyler's breathing. He stood there like a wrestler, waiting for his opponent to get up so that he could floor him again. Conway was already experiencing the first wave of consternation. He had seen the hammer blow and had been in front of Chandler, with a view of his face when he fell. The scientist was the first to move. He knelt beside the wreckage and felt for a pulse. Without a word he then hurried from the room and returned at once with a mirror which he held to Chandler's mouth. At that point Tyler crouched down and also felt for a pulse. The mirror remained bright.

The last vestige of colour drained from Conway's face. "He's dead," he whispered.

At first Tyler seemed not to believe it but then he stood up, abruptly, and turned away. There was a wide cornice above the old-fashioned fireplace and he gripped it in both hands with his back to the room. For a time he was very still but then his shoulders heaved in a series of deep breaths and he seemed to relax. When he turned round he gave Conway a further jolt by being perfectly composed. "All right then. He's dead," he said briskly. "We can't put the clock back, so we must decide what to do next."

Conway just gaped at him, unable to think at all. The whisky bottle, which had been on the coffee table, had rolled away unbroken. Tyler fetched glasses and poured two ample measures. "Come on, drink it. We can't leave things like this for long. *Something* has to be done." He watched Conway impatiently as he gulped and swallowed obediently.

"What can we do? It's police business now."

"That's all the more reason why we must think. Now let's take this one thing at a time. You came home to find your house broken into, right?"

Conway nodded. "It's easy to get in, really. The front door was locked, though. It has to be; it swings open if it's not."

"Good. So where would he have got in?"

Conway's shoulders lifted slightly. "Anywhere. They are all sash windows; easy enough to slide up from outside." He seemed to draw some confidence from talking about simple, factual matters and Tyler followed up the lead.

"There you are then. You come home to find that Chandler has broken into your home and when we confront him he gets violent. We try to restrain him but in all the heat and confusion we overdo it. We are talking about using unnecessary force in the heat of the moment. That's very understandable surely."

"Yes but . . . the enquiries. All the investigating and questioning. They'll need to know every detail; everything that happened, everything that was said. There will have to be newspaper reports. It won't sound the way you put it. They might even think that we had to . . . to stop him."

81

"Could it really be taken that seriously, what you're doing up there? Is it conceivable that you would be that desperate because of what he knew?"

Conway did not reply.

"Come on, nobody's going to believe that you'd want him killed because he found out about your little sideline."

"Not killed, no not that. But . . . stopped. It will be the other way round then, you see. I'll be the guilty one not him. It won't be as if we caught a burglar at all. It will be as if I had been caught in the wrong. That's how it was really and that's how they'll make it sound."

"Well we'll just have to make bloody sure they don't, won't we. We have to be able to explain this as a regrettable, tragic accident during a struggle with a man who had no right to be here. No way did we want him hurt; we had no motive. No motive at all. You just have to make sure that nobody can find any motive. It shouldn't be that difficult if he was the only one who knew anything."

"He said something about evidence," Conway said hesitantly.

Their eyes were drawn to the dead man as their thoughts coincided.

"All right," Tyler said. "I'll check his pockets; you check the car."

Conway watched him search the jacket and the trouser pockets that he could get to. Next he heaved at the shoulders to roll the body over. At first Conway did not realize what he was seeing as Chandler's chest came into view. The shirt front was wet. There was very little blood. Death had been caused by damage to the spinal cord at the base of the skull, in effect, a broken neck. And then Conway understood and cried out in horror. "Don't touch it!" And he hurried from the room.

Using rubber gloves and stainless steel tongs from his laboratory Conway probed the breast pocket. His hands were shaking. He brought out two small glass phials and some large fragments. The phials bore numbers marked in felt pen. Parts of numbers and lettering could also be seen on the fragments. Four other phials were found, intact, in a side pocket. Conway slowly raised his head. "You'll find empty glass jars and thick plastic bags upstairs on a shelf. Left hand side as you go in." His voice was barely audible.

"What is it?"

"Please . . ."

When Tyler came back Conway sealed up the phials and pieces of glass and covered the wet area. Then he sealed up the tongs and gloves in plastic bags.

"What is all this?"

"It couldn't be worse; there's no hope for us now."

"Look, for Christ's sake pull yourself together. What is it?"

It took a little time and more whisky but eventually Tyler got his explanation. "They were from my sub-samples. Cultures. All viruses. It must have broken when he hit the table. It's a neurotropic one — like rabies. They invade nerve cells normally but this is an experimental form produced by selection. I needed to emphasize the processes I was studying, you see."

"You mean it's a sort of super virus."

"Like that, yes. It's highly invasive. It will even pass through cornified tiss . . . through skin. From the nerve endings it travels to the central nervous system. It will always be lethal."

Tyler stared at him incredulously. "And you had this sort of stuff lying about upstairs?"

"No! No, of course not. The house was locked, the lab was locked and I kept all the phials in an old safe. He must have been an expert on locks. He must have been."

Tyler just shook his head, at a loss for words.

"Don't you see?" Conway went on. "It really couldn't be worse. If you hadn't killed him he would have died anyway. And we couldn't have let him go. He could have started an epidemic. Now they'll be certain that we wanted him dead."

"But can't you do something about it? Clean it off or something?"

"It's too late now. I couldn't destroy the virus at this stage without it showing. He could be infective for days."

For some time neither of them spoke. Tyler paced the room and at one point he walked through to the back of the house and looked outside. When he came back he paced for a few moments more and then he said "We still have a chance. If he just disappears there probably won't be too much hue and cry. People disappear every day. I've read the figures. Most of them intend to vanish: money problems, women problems. Unless there's reason to suspect something the police don't pull out all the stops. It just becomes another name on the missing persons list. Was he married?"

"No, but I don't know much about his personal life. I only knew him at work."

"Well we'll just have to hope he lived a fast life and was up to his ears in debt."

"Keith, we haven't a hope of getting away with it. He might have told somebody where he was going and in any case his car's outside. People might have seen it there."

"I have thought about that and I say there's a chance. Even if it's only a slim chance it's worth taking. We haven't much to lose now."

"But the questioning. I couldn't face it."

"You'll have to face it one way or the other unless you try to disappear yourself."

Conway shook his head hopelessly. "Where could I go right now, tonight?"

"Exactly. You need time to plan. We both do. Remember, Chandler will simply have gone, vanished, whereabouts unknown, like thousands of others. Nobody is going to suspect you of anything. If you are asked you say, 'Sure he was here. He brought this book back. He seemed a bit odd but nothing too unusual. When he left I assumed he was going home.' You can give them all the right times except that it will be me going off in his car, not him. The mist has thickened so when his car drives away nobody is going to see who's driving it. If anyone sees or hears it leaving then so much the better. Nobody knows I'm here so I can clear out and take his car at the same time. I know where I can take it. It won't be found again."

"Yes but what about . . . him?"

Tyler had thought about that as well.

It was nearly six months later that Conway discovered, quite by accident, another unique property of the virus that had so nearly put him in prison.

SEVEN

"THERE ISN'T GOING to be an easy way, according to Daintry."

"Well, he would know, Bill. He's cracked some hard ones in his time."

"Just hasn't enough to work on, he says. Doesn't even know enough for a convincing bluff."

"So what does he suggest?"

"He has less than 24 hours to go, but the Home Office and the magistrates are usually pretty co-operative in cases like this so he thinks he could get an extension. The trouble is, he's not sure it will do any good. If Tyler doesn't crack within the next day or so he probably won't cave in at all. Once the extension is up, of course, he'll just have to be turned loose again. Daintry is willing to help out with continued surveillance but you know how it is with long jobs: down to one trainee every time they're short of legmen."

"I know, I know." Randolph sighed and studied the ceiling. "I wish Daintry felt more confident. It would have made things so much easier. I suppose it was too much to hope for. The thing is that if we are going to end up with a phase two operation sooner or later, then it ought to be sooner."

"Of course."

Randolph smiled faintly. "Sorry, Bill. I was thinking aloud. But to think a little further, what do we tell de Wet?"

Fletcher promptly removed his pipe to speak but then paused. "Oh, I see what you mean. We will have to tell him something won't we."

"I'm afraid so. He will know as well as we do what can be done under the P of T Act. He'll allow five days for maximum extension and then he will know that Tyler has either been charged or released. There would be no point in trying to keep it quiet."

"Of course they do have a third option in South African prisons. We could try saying that he hung himself with his socks."

Randolph ignored that. "We are simply going to have to bring them in on it, Bill. The only alternative is to say outright that we have decided to keep this one to ourselves." He shook his head even as he spoke. "They wouldn't stand for it. They'd hit us back over there. We're too vulnerable."

"Oh, I know that, James. What you say is true. I just like to kick a bit when I'm cornered that's all. I'll admit, though, that when we worked out a plan for phase two I hadn't seriously considered having the *Jaaps* breathing down our necks.

"It ought not to make too much difference. It will still be our show though I suppose they'll want to put somebody at the ringside."

"With our fieldmen?" Indignation appeared on his podgy face.

"Well it will only be a watching brief."

"I should bloody well hope so. Have you decided who gets the main part?"

"I've thought about it quite a lot but I haven't actually done anything about it yet. How do you assess the risk in this? To our man, I mean."

Fletcher waved his pipe as if to dismiss the idea. "Nothing to it as far as I can see. Dammit he'll be on home ground with a British national under our supervision. Can't be tucked up much safer than that."

Randolph nodded his white head very slowly but his light blue eyes seemed clouded by uncertainty when he said, "Yes, it ought to be secure, I agree."

"I favour giving Lawson a chance with this one."

"Because you think it's an easy assignment?"

"I didn't say it would be easy; just relatively safe. And I believe Lawson could handle it. He fits the part."

"He still has no experience."

"Well he has to start somewhere and he's done a pretty comprehensive training. What's bothering you, James? You'd rather break him in as part of a team, is that it? It isn't the way you usually think. You'd have the whole team to worry about then. If you are worried, that is."

"No, no, I agree with you. It's just that I like to have a contingency plan, or preferably two. As it is I feel less than prepared. This may be only a cosy little operation on home ground, Bill, but it's all rather openended and unpredictable. I mean, we don't know where or what it's going to lead to, do we?"

Fletcher had no reply.

Interrogation, without the use of physical or chemical persuasion, is an art. Bullying brings results from some but makes others more intransigent. There are those who can be coaxed, those who can be conned and some who are open to reason. But in every case it helps if the interrogator knows something to start with because confirmation comes a lot easier than information.

Daintry's man, an old hand called Bryce, knew very little. The South Africans had let it be assumed that their information was obtained entirely through informers. Illicit tape recordings, tactfully, had not been mentioned by either side. The circumstances were far from satisfactory for an arrest and interrogation, but it wasn't the first time that arrests had been made out of expediency and it wouldn't be the last. That was what Section 12 was all about — it gave the boys in blue, or out of it, a chance to get into the game. Bryce determined to make the most of it.

"Where did you meet him?"

"In a pub."

"Which pub?"

"I don't remember."

"When was it?"

"About a month ago."

"And you can't remember?"

"Well, I'd been in a few pubs, had a few drinks . . ."

"So how did you remember about the meeting? Saw him again did you?"

"I remembered it, that's all."

"You mean you were too pissed to remember where you were but you didn't forget the arrangements you made?"

"I just remembered it."

"Why did you go to his office, then?"

"I didn't go to his office."

"We have already established that you did."

"Oh, well, that was after. That was the arrangement you see. He asked me to call at his office."

87

"Why?"

"To meet this friend of his."

"What did you talk about in his office?"

"Nothing. His friend didn't turn up so I just waited a bit and then left."

"So when did you arrange to meet him down the tube?"

"I phoned him later to see if he'd heard anything and that's when he said he would meet me at the station."

"Why did you leave South Africa?"

Tyler shrugged, thinking desperately. "I didn't much like it there."

"Why not?"

"I didn't like being away from home."

"You didn't like the politics?"

"Yes, no, I'm not interested in politics."

"The Free Africa Movement *is* bloody politics. You couldn't talk to Gabriel Tamala about anything else."

"I know that, I know, but I'm not really interested. We just got talking in the pub, that's all."

"Why go to meet his friend then? Why go to his office? Why phone up? Why go down the tube after him?"

"He asked me to. He said it was important, so I went."

"And this friend he introduced you to without giving any name, what was his accent like?"

"He didn't have much of an accent. European, I think."

"Christ, we know who he is. I just want to hear you describe his accent to see if you can tell the truth about anything. Now, was he French, German, Irish, South African?"

"No, not South African. European of some sort."

"What did you talk about?"

"I've told you, he . . ."

"Tell me again."

Tyler did and got it nearly word perfect, explaining that they'd asked him where he worked and whom he had known in South Africa.

"Why would they ask you that?"

"I suppose they're always looking for useful contacts."

"What are they paying?"

"I don't know. We never talked about money. I had nothing to sell."

"Nothing to sell and no interest in politics. It's not what they are saying about you, and their story is going to sound a bloody sight more believable in court. You're letting two foreigners sew you up on your own patch, you stupid bugger. Now write down all the names of people you knew in South Africa."

"But I've done that. I can't think of any more."

"Good. It won't take you long then. Just write them down. We're interested in the ones you miss out."

It was true that Bryce knew who Tamala's friend was but it was little help to him because the said gentleman had a diplomatic passport. As a cultural liaison officer he came under embassy administration without actually being on the embassy staff. Moscow was pleased to protect such useful citizens with special passports and the British, to Bryce's disgust, were soft enough to wear it. Gabriel Tamala had no such protection. His South African travel documents had long since been withdrawn and he lived in London because he had been granted political asylum in the UK. He was far from being untouchable, but one had to tread very carefully with people like Mr Tamala; they could command instant sympathy and enthusiastic attention from a large section of the British press. For starters, Bryce had no one but Tyler to work on.

"Why you? Why should they approach you when you have such a tiny circle of friends and no interest in politics?"

"I don't know. We just got . . ."

"Talking in a pub, you've told me. When did you last see your mother?"

"Not all that long ago. Six or eight weeks."

"She's worried about you. She says she sees very little of you these days. Says you've changed. Why have you changed? What's different?"

Tyler's throat tightened at the mention of his mother. How far back would they go? Would she mention the weekend that he was supposed to stay and didn't? She had been upset about it. He had intended to phone her from Conway's house and if things had gone normally that night he would have done. He rubbed his forehead wearily, hoping to hide his moment of fear. When he looked up again his pale eyes held no more expression than those of a dead fish but Bryce had noticed. He had found a chink but did not know how to interpret it. The *mother*?

"Very fond of your mother, are you?"

"Yes, of course."

"Why don't you see more of her then?"

"I keep in touch by phone. I ought to get up there more often, it's true, but it costs money to keep going to Stoke."

The mother. How the hell to tie in the mother. Perhaps he had a thing about her. Oedipus Tyler. There was a pressure point there, he was certain of it, but was it relevant? Bryce decided to store it for the time being.

"Last weekend, before we brought you in, what did you do? Where did you go?"

"I didn't go anywhere. I put a new radiator in the car."

"All weekend for a job like that?"

"I couldn't get the old one out. The bolts were all rusty. I cleaned up the old water pump as well; you can check."

"Oh, we are doing. We're checking with your neighbours and everybody you've ever spoken to from your mother onwards. And then we're going to put your signed statement up against all the rest — that's why I keep giving you a chance to change your story. Now then, we'll try again: what did you talk about at your little tête-à-tête in the Underground? And I might just play you a tape-recording afterwards to go with your photographs." Bryce was very reluctant to use the tape. The quality was abysmal. As evidence it was useless and as a show of strength it revealed far too much weakness. But he needed a bluff.

Tyler felt a lurch of panic but suppressed it with dogged fortitude. "Tamala had told his friend what I'd been doing in South Africa. He wanted more details. I told him where I worked and about the people there and what I did. He seemed disappointed. There was nothing to interest him. I knew there wouldn't be."

"Why do you think your friends tell a different story to yours?"

"I don't know; they must be trying to put the blame on me."

"Blame for what? What have they done?"

"I can't imagine but they must have done something to cause all this trouble."

"Tell me again about the work you did in South Africa."

"I was a chemist, well, assistant really. I was testing most of the time. When they come up with a new product that passes all the lab tests they put it out for field trials. As I told you, I was testing fly-strike treatment in sheep for about a year. After that I went on to . . ."

"What else besides veterinary products?"

"Nothing. Ask Pharmatech."

Special Branch already had the report that Meester had compiled. It was no help. Slowly he shook his head. "It seems to me, Tyler, that you are determined to give your mother real cause for worry." He had him taken back to the cells with a parting shot about trying to get more sense from the old lady.

"Sheep," he muttered as Tyler was led away.

Later that afternoon Daintry, Randolph and Fletcher reached their decision on phase two of the operation.

It is an established fact, as well as common experience, that the human psyche is at its lowest ebb at three o'clock in the morning. At that hour, by the biological clock, the brain is least able to cope with inputs and demands from the outside world. Tyler was sleeping fitfully when the demand reached his grey matter so there was also an element of surprise and bewilderment to add to the mental overload.

"Tyler, wake up. Come on, man, move it!"

"Why? What . . ."

"Don't talk, just get these on quick." A bundle hit him in the chest as he blinked at the policeman in the dim light. He registered the fact that it was a bundle of clothes and that the blankets had already been dragged off his bed. Suddenly he was awake and doing as he was told, fumbling at the buttons of the shirt and struggling into loose, unfamiliar trousers.

"What's happening? What time is it?"

"I said don't talk, just speed it up for Christ's sake." He grabbed the shoes, finding that they were slip-ons without laces. He pulled on a thick jersey and felt it tugged roughly over his head from the back before a strong hand seized his arm and pushed him towards the door.

The corridor outside was lit by a solitary night-light and as he was hustled past the other cells in the little block Tyler could see, dimly, the one other inmate. He was sprawled diagonally across the narrow bunk, his head against the wall and one leg hanging over the side. His snores reverberated around the bare walls. Earlier, when they had brought him in, he had been a lot noisier.

There was a security door at the end of the passage which had been unlocked and relocked on Tyler's arrival. Now it was ajar and he sent it crashing against the wall with his free arm as the man behind frog-marched him through without a pause. Nor was there very much time for Tyler to take in the astonishing scene ahead. It was to be expected that the station would be quiet at that hour, commotions were at a 24 hour low, but the tableau which confronted him was all the more dramatic for being absolutely silent.

The duty sergeant was a grim statue with his fingers linked above his head. The young wireless operator stood beside him, also against the wall, looking shocked. Two others stared at the floor. All had their hands above their heads and none moved. In front of the line-up a bearded man in a faded blue suit covered them with what looked like a sawn-off shotgun. Two other men, one of them in police uniform, the other in blue jeans and a pullover, stood just inside the outer door, obviously intensely anxious. As Tyler gaped it was the one in uniform who broke the silence.

"Be quick, for Christ's sake, they'll all be here any minute."

The one holding Tyler had scarcely hesitated but now he shoved forward so hard that Tyler stumbled and nearly fell.

"There's nobody down there except some stinking drunk. Lock them in while we get mobile."

Shotgun was already moving the line towards the cells as Tyler and his escort reached the outer door. At that moment the two door-guards became wild eyed.

"There's one here now; just drawn up!"

Tyler felt the grip on his arm tighten as he was pulled aside. Seconds later the door swung open and the first of two patrolmen came in. He was still talking to the one behind as he stepped into the room. Then he looked at Tyler and his eyes, puzzled, switched to the face beyond, then to the uniformed man. The uncertainty was fleeting but it gave time for the other patrolman to come inside. The door-guards then went into action. Their hands were already concealing tiny black aerosol cylinders and they used them simultaneously. The patrolmen moved quickly but they were not fast enough. Tyler actually saw a fine jet form beads on the back of one man's hand and on the side of his face. He ducked and gasped as his eyes began to stream. One of them shouted out and was silenced by a blow from behind. Tyler saw both patrolmen being hit while he, himself, was being hustled through the doorway and into the street.

They pushed him into the back seat of a waiting car and were moving off when the other one in police uniform ran from the station and heaved himself in.

"Come on, foot down," he panted. "I think it was just chance that those two checked in. I don't believe they even knew the radio was out. But others will by now." As he spoke he pulled off his hat and tunic and stuffed them under the seat. Tyler's escort did the same. They swept past the barracks and on to Prince Albert Road, turning right into Primrose Hill where they pulled up abruptly.

"Right. Out! Well, come on — out, out!"

Once again Tyler found himself being pushed and chivvied across the pavement and through a door. The car sped away towards the railway bridge and the maze of small streets beyond.

It was a dingy room which smelled faintly of urine. The furniture was old and a shabby quilt had been pulled over an obviously unmade bed. It could have been the bedsitter of someone aged and infirm whose last years were being spent in poverty. But a collection of grubby paperbacks suggested otherwise. Whoever lived there was probably well within his reproductive years.

"We'll be safe here for a bit. We can move on when the streets are busy."

As the man spoke Tyler had his first thorough look at him. He was in his early to mid thirties, tall and evidently strong without being bulky. His eyes and hair were middle brown and his complexion fresh. Tyler considered him to be quite good looking though not strikingly handsome. There was nothing particularly memorable about his features; his face was just a successful combination of all its parts. The precise set of the eyes, such a strongly individual characteristic, was in fact greatly influenced by a slight thickening between the eyes and the bridge of the nose, but this would be apparent only to an experienced analyst such as a portrait artist or one trained in those perceptive skills. Similarly, a tightening of the tissue at either side of the chin was responsible for the involuntary set of the mouth. A slight cleft in the chin itself was another contributory factor. The lobes of the ears were neatly rounded and a distinct flaring of the nostrils was evident in profile. It never occurred to Tyler that the face was anything but natural as it registered relief from the strain of the past timeless minutes. It never entered his head that the face could be, in large measure, a product of the surgeon's art.

"What do I call you?" he asked.

The other seemed to consider for a moment, then he said "Peter."

"Just Peter?"

"It's enough isn't it? You can call me Peter the Great if you like."

"Am I allowed to ask now what the hell is going on?"

"I'd have thought, by now, it was obvious. Just think yourself lucky they only kept you in the local lock-up and not a high security place."

"Lucky! I could have walked out of Albany Street tomorrow, legally. They'd have had to let me go. I was holding out — no problem. They weren't getting anywhere with me."

"You're not being very bright, my friend. Suppose they had let you go. What then? Did you think you could just carry on where you left off? Did you think you only needed to tell Tamala you were back in business? You are a Special Branch suspect now, a bad smell at the party. Nobody wants to be connected."

"I could have waited until the heat was off," Tyler said uncertainly.

"It will never be off. They don't really set you free when their time is up, you know. They put you back over the side but they still have you on a line. They can pull you in again any time they think is right. You're on computer file — automatic entries every time you fill in a form or sign a cheque. Your phone could be tapped, your mail could be read, you'd have a shadow for certain. But now, the way we have it, they have to find you first."

"Well I still have to live, don't I? I still need banks, driving licence, phone calls, a name and address, applications for . . ."

"These things can all be arranged given time and money. The main thing is to be able to disappear to start with. That's what you can't do by walking out of the police cells when they open the door for you."

Tyler was silent for a while, then he said, "It isn't only that is it? It isn't just me. You were afraid I was a risk to certain other people. You knew I hadn't talked because the ripples weren't spreading but you couldn't stand the suspense. At the very least you thought I would tell them what I was selling, what I'd arranged with your people and the deal would be off. Well I told them nothing and I still say I could have walked out of there and then disappeared. As it is there will be a major bloody manhunt and I'm in bigger trouble. There's no way I can play the innocent if they pick me up now. But that's just what you want isn't it?" Tyler warmed to his theme as he saw more of the implications. "That's exactly what you want. You've got me by the balls. I'm dependent on you to get me out of this and it just so happens that you want what I have to sell. You've made two smart moves in one haven't you? You've got me safely where I'm no risk and I'm in no bloody bargaining position either!"

Peter stretched himself on the bed and sighed impatiently. "Think what you like then. But when you've thought it through you'll realize that this way you still have your options open. Any other way and you'd be out in the cold. I told you, with Special Branch breathing down your neck nobody wants to know you."

After that they did not speak for some time. Tyler paced about nervously and at one point went over to the window and peered out through the grimy curtains.

"Come away from there. With that red hair you might as well wave a flag. It's the first thing we have to cover up before we leave here."

Tyler, sullenly, did as he was told. The more he thought, the more he realized how serious his position had become. He felt a flood of new worries and fears. "I don't think we'll get away with this. They'll be really stirred up now. For all you know they might have picked up the car already."

"They probably have but it won't do them any good. It was just a car off a car park. And there was another car swap laid on within minutes of here. They'll be lying up now like us. Not very far away. We are not exactly amateurs, you know."

"What was it they squirted the police with?"

"Chemical Mace. Haven't you seen it before?"

"No."

"Smith and Wesson make it. It's illegal in the UK but in New York everybody has one. Women carry them in their handbags because of all the muggers and rapists."

"But what does it do? I mean, how serious is it?"

"It's not serious. It wears off after a while."

"They didn't need to hit them as well."

"Listen; for Christ' sake stop wailing, will you? You're out aren't you? We couldn't ponce up and down at a time like that. Nobody's been killed."

"I just hope not, that's all." And then, as if on an afterthought. "Are you English?"

"Sure I'm English. Don't I look English?"

Tyler shrugged. "I just want to know who I'm dealing with, that's all."

"You'll never know that. You aren't intended to. We got you out because your friend Tamala knows some powerful, wealthy people. Or maybe he doesn't know them either. It's results that count. You don't need names."

"Where is Tamala now? Are they still holding him?"

"He hasn't been held. They questioned him a few times but they didn't keep him in. They'll be watching him though, like a hawk now that you are out. They'll be watching everybody you ever knew."

"From my mother onwards," Tyler murmured.

"What? Sure, everybody."

"Why did they pick me up in the first place? I mean, what did they have to go on?"

"That's what we'd all like to know. They were watching one of you, must have been. When you had your meeting they got curious and pulled you in."

"The other one, the East European or whatever he was. They said they knew him. Would they be watching him? Who was he?"

"I don't know who was handling you before. I don't want to know. They'll release the money through me when you come up with the goods."

"There's more to think about now."

"Well, don't take too long about it. It's not just money we have to find. You need documents, tickets, you need help."

"I could see that to begin with, couldn't I?"

"Well it's up to you but I can't wait forever. Anyway, see if you can find some coffee, we have hours to wait in this place yet."

Moving Tyler to a safe house in the south suburbs was no great hazard. There was little risk from the general public because the news release had been deliberately low key, though true enough in its essentials. Tyler himself heard it later that day:

A man escaped, this morning, from Albany Street Police station where he was being held in custody. The man, Keith Tyler, was helping police with their enquiries into suspected terrorist links between mainland Britain and certain undisclosed centres abroad. A police spokesman said the man escaped with the help of accomplices. He is thirty and is described as being a little over six feet tall and of slim build. At the time of his escape he was wearing a dark brown pullover and fawn trousers. He is not considered to be dangerous.

Tyler swallowed hard. The sound of his own name on the lips of the newsreader affected him deeply. Somehow it was as if the report was a measure of the gravity of his situation, a rating in the public concern charts. "They didn't give much detail, did they?"

"I don't suppose they feel very proud of being locked in their own cells. They wouldn't announce it if they didn't have to."

"They didn't say anybody had been hurt."

"I told you nobody was hurt. Not much anyway."

"I wonder why they didn't mention my hair. I'd expect it to be the first thing they'd think of. You know, as a distinguishing feature."

"They probably expect you to dye it."

"But they must expect me to change my clothes. Why mention that?"

Peter shrugged as if it were of no importance. "It's just a news report. It might be only half of what the police told them. Maybe there will be a full description in the papers; photographs even."

"I should dye this hair now. Can you get some hair dye?"

"I'll try but they'll be expecting that. It's best if I get a woman to buy it."

"Are you married?"

Tyler thought he noticed a slight change of expression in Peter's eyes — as if a raw nerve had been touched. But all he said was "no".

Tyler did not question the wisdom of keeping himself out of sight while Peter went out to get food and other essentials. He had no fear of being abandoned by those he was dealing with. But nor was he under any illusions about their integrity. They were as criminal as he was. If they could get what they wanted without paying they would dump him without a second thought. There would be nothing he could do about it.

Providing them with another sample ought to be safe enough. It could be arranged over the telephone and with fifty thousand in cash he would feel less helpless. It had to be the first move. He had been clear of the police for nearly eighteen hours and tension had given some way to tiredness but he was also beginning to worry about Conway. Had things gone according to plan he would have phoned Ralph after the meeting on the underground. Having heard nothing, Ralph's disposition would have got the better of him. He would have been scared and worried out of his mind. Now he would have heard the news report and would be desperate to know whether he had been exposed to the police. When Peter came back, Tyler resolved, hair dye or not, he would have to go out to find a phone box.

EIGHT

WHEN JAMES RANDOLPH returned to his office late that afternoon he had a quiet, abstracted air which somehow made him look physically smaller and more fragile. He placed his briefcase carefully beside his desk and pushed aside the memo pad with a single finger. "Tell me, Bill, what's been happening at this end?"

Whether or not he was aware of it Fletcher always responded to his senior's more reserved moods by becoming slightly louder. "Everything's still on hold," he said heartily. "No problems with the surveillance. Lawson came out to report. Tyler hasn't shown. Do you want to hear the report now?"

"Oh, not if it's only a contact call. Sounds all right doesn't he?"

"Sounds fine. Absolutely certain that Tyler suspects nothing but he says he's not pushing him. Nothing that we didn't already know, of course. Daintry's chaps seem to have gone overboard with their eavesdropping: they've even got the lavatory coming over, er, loud and clear."

Randolph raised his eyebrows.

"Tell me, James," Fletcher went on, "how did you get on with our friends from Trafalgar Square?"

"De Wet wasn't too pleased. He thinks we've kept him less than well-informed."

"Expected to be told things in advance, did he?"

"That's not what he said. He's annoyed because he considers that he handed this thing over to us and now we're being all possessive about it."

"My heart bleeds for him. What did he expect?"

"I rather think he expected more collaboration: thought we might have discussed our contingency plans with him instead of just turning Tyler loose and then telling him."

Fletcher shrugged. "Better than not telling him. How much did you let him have in the end?"

"It went almost exactly as we predicted. He asked all the awkward questions, didn't miss any out, and I told him everything except where Tyler is now. He told me what he thought of us and we left it at that."

"Don't call us, we'll call you." Fletcher looked at his watch, stood up and stifled a yawn. "I think I'll go home, James. This may be the lull before a storm; might as well use it."

Randolph nodded, his thoughts elsewhere. "I wonder how much he really knows," he murmured.

Fletcher sat down again. "About what, exactly?"

"He's afraid that Tyler will manage to pull off this deal and yet he still insists that he has no idea what it is he's trying to sell."

"Could be true. After all, if he's stuck his neck out by coming to us without clearance from his own superiors, he's not going to feel too comfortable whatever he knows — or doesn't know."

"I suppose not. He came to us on his own initiative, I'm certain of it. I also feel sure that he was bending the rules when he got on to this business and I wouldn't be surprised if he's holding something back." He produced a quick little smile. "It probably makes no difference. Weren't you going home?"

Bill Fletcher made no move. "What you mean is, you *hope* it makes no difference. What you are afraid of, I see now, is that Lawson might be up against more than we're prepared for; de Wet knows it and that's what's bothering the little bugger. Did you ask him outright?"

"Yes."

"Well if Lawson comes to grief and de Wet could have prevented it I'll personally have his balls."

"You like Peter Lawson, don't you?"

"I value him. You saw his potential first and as usual you were right. He showed more enterprise and competence on the wrong side of the law than some I can think of who have worked for us. It was your idea to bring him across for training; give us a chance to study him and see if he would measure up. That sort of recruitment only happens in story books, James. It's a fairy-tale. It's the way Robin Hood might have got his men. We need a case like that, now and then, in our game. It's a sort of restorative. I want it to be a success story."

In the Cambridgeshire village of Ketley, Ralph Conway shivered slightly in his bleak kitchen and stirred mechanically at a pan of rice and mince. At his feet a mongrel puppy was watching him intently and sweeping an arc of faded tiling with its tail. It was the second day that Conway had not been to work. Tomorrow he would need a doctor's certificate. It was a visit that he dreaded but knew he could not avoid. More important than sick pay was the fact that unexplained absences would arouse curiosity at the laboratory; interest, enquiries. Better to face the questions of a country practitioner who would be content with symptoms and a guess at the cause. You need a holiday, he might say. Been overworking, perhaps.

Conway drew a deep breath, unevenly, like a slight shudder. "If only they knew," he murmured to the dog, and the puppy switched its tail in a higher gear and shuffled forward, whimpering with anticipation.

Chronic stress, he knew well, was a case of the mind affecting the body. Clinically the condition was complex: a chain reaction from the thinking brain through the pituitary to the adrenal glands. Hormones from the adrenal cortex kept up the constant message — you are under stress — under stress — under stress. The very chemistry of one's blood was altered as part of the whole complicated syndrome. The only real cure was to remove the cause of the anxiety. The only ones with resistance to the disease were those who did not worry. Experimentally, animals can be killed by stress. Take a holiday old chap. If only they knew.

It was the feeling of helplessness which came most strongly into Conway's consciousness; the frustration of having to wait passively for release. He had missed the brief news report, and again and again he stared at the telephone and at the number that Tyler had given to him. Only as a last resort, Keith had said. If anything happens to me take it from there but don't contact them unless you have to. That way you won't exist in this affair and that's the safest situation for both of us. It was a situation that Conway was afraid to change but, as the days passed without word from his friend, the burden of doing nothing became unbearable.

He made the call at four o'clock that afternoon and at least retained enough presence of mind to refer to his friend only as Smith.

Gabriel Tamala hesitated before making any reply at all and when he did it was very cautiously. "Who are you? Are you a friend of his? A colleague?"

"As I said, he told me he would be seeing you on a business matter. He told me to contact you if he did not get back in touch with me immediately afterwards. That was five days ago. I am making enquiries, Mr Tamala. I am hoping to avoid off . . ." He swallowed on the syllable, "official channels, you see. You will understand that."

"Yes. Yes, of course. We don't want to cause unnecessary trouble but I have not heard from him either. I will also make enquiries. I will see what I can find out but where do I contact you, Mr, er . . . ?"

"I will call you back."

Conway rattled down the receiver with a shaking hand. He had not known what to expect from the call but the over-cautious response had done nothing to reassure him. Something had gone wrong and Keith Tyler, who had become Conway's mainstay in life, had disappeared. For a while he experienced total desolation. He had survived the past months on the hope that Tyler's scheme would succeed and they would become rich. Rich enough to buy a new life somewhere safe from the old one. The hope of a fresh start had sustained Ralph Conway and held off the breakdown that had threatened him for more than a year. At first he had expected the tension to ease with time. He had thought, wishfully, that the passage of time alone would bring reassurance and a sense of greater security. But after the initial panic had subsided there remained a gnawing fear of discovery which never seemed to diminish and which accumulated in his system like a slow poison. Now, alone, he was to face another crisis and he knew that he was not up to it.

The certain knowledge that he would rather die than continue as he was, came to the scientist as a revelation.

From the very lowest ebb of his spirit he saw clearly that he was more afraid of being discovered than of death itself. He was surprised to find a trace of comfort in it. The worst need never happen. There was a way out which would be easier for him. The acceptance of that fact must become his new support. He must take strength from it, depend on it, make it dependable. The worst need never happen. Very slowly Conway walked through the kitchen to the back door. The puppy, now nudging the empty tin plate across the floor, scarcely gave him a glance.

Outside, near the wall, a roll of rusted wire netting lay upon a few sheets of roofing iron — the remnants, he had always supposed, of an old chicken coop. He dragged them aside and, ignoring the cockroaches which scuttled in the sudden light, he reached for an iron ring in the trapdoor to the cellar. It was at that moment that someone rapped the heavy knocker on the front door. Conway drew back, his heart pounding. Although he stood alone in his neglected garden he looked like a man who could not explain his own presence. He thought he heard voices but could not be sure; the dog was barking indoors. The knocking came again and this time he went towards it as if he were under hypnosis.

There was an old gate between the hedge and the corner of the house. The hinges had gone and it was wired to a post on both sides. From there he could see the front door and the visitor could see him.

"Oh, hello." The girl smiled hesitantly, her plump cheeks radiating health. "We're collecting in aid of the old folk." Her companion hung back a foot or two. "Shelter," she added, and tossed the coins in the box she was holding. Conway stared down at it, at the slot in the circular lid, the girl's green woollen glove with the red band at the wrist. He looked past her to the shining scooter which was parked on the little green. His lips moved to say "of course" but no sound came. He produced some coins and dropped them in.

"Thank you very much. Thank you." They trod back to the gate and he watched them pick their way between the puddles. They looked carefree and comfortable; happy bundles of woollies and scarves. The air was clear but sharp and in the open a chill breeze was blowing. Conway turned from the corner into the lee of the house and the overgrown garden. He felt quite ill.

It was a narrow cellar with plastered walls and an earth-stained floor of bricks without mortar. Propped at one end was a set of old window-frames with grimy glass. Part of an old fireplace stood in front of them, and an aquarium with a side missing. Seed boxes filled with lifeless soil had once, many years before, produced a few mushrooms. Rows of dusty bottles stood on planks raised off the floor. A few of them had corks but most were empty. Conway crouched at the top of the short ladder for several minutes. It was the first time he had opened the trapdoor for nearly a year but the details of that dismal pit were burned in his memory and he had seen and breathed it a thousand times. For four hours he had toiled there, alone, after Tyler had gone in Chandler's car. It had been Tyler who had carried the weight of Chandler's body; tumbled it roughly into its crypt. But Conway had done nothing to try to stop him. He had wanted to believe that Tyler's way might offer a chance. It was for Conway the proverbial straw on the water. And then it had been too late. After an hour or a year the truth can only be confession.

He had waited until daylight that Sunday morning, afraid of showing light. Before midday the soil had been scattered among the weeds of his garden and the bricks had been relaid in the cellar floor, coated as before with dust and earth. He looked down now, fearfully, but there was nothing to see. Nothing had changed.

From the bottom of the ladder he stared up at the hinges in the heavy wood and at the surrounding structure. Mentally he measured the distance which the trapdoor would move before clearing its frame. He gazed around the walls as if he were trapped but the escape he was contemplating was of an entirely different kind. He made no movement beyond the slow turn of his upraised head. The sky was framed less than two feet above him but the air had the stillness of a sealed chamber. When he had seen enough he climbed quietly back to the surface and suddenly his enclosed little garden seemed to be vibrant with breeze and movement and noise.

Half an hour later he was pondering his plan for the cellar when the telephone rang. It was Tyler, to tell him there was nothing to worry about.

"Nothing to worry about?" Conway echoed shrilly. "My God, Keith, it's seemed like weeks. What's been happening? Where are you? Why couldn't you have called before if there's nothing to worry about?"

"I can't explain now. There was a problem but not any more. I thought you would have heard. Things are moving along again; don't worry."

"But why didn't you call me before?"

"I'll explain when I see you. I can't tell you on the phone." A note of irritation crept into Tyler's voice.

"And when is that likely to be?" Conway became sullen in response.

"Not long. We are on the home straight, now. But, Ralph, we need another sample. It will speed things up." Tyler recognized the need for reassurance and quickly regretted having sounded impatient. "Please don't worry; it really is all right now. Can you get another sample to me quickly?"

In all the fears and doubts which had racked Conway's mind for the past twelve months there had been not a germ of suspicion or distrust towards his friend. Now, almost subconsciously, there fell the first cast of doubt. "Why do they need another sample? It will only be the same as before."

"I know that. It's what I said. In fact, at first I refused because I felt they were just trying to play games with us. But then I asked for 10 per cent on it and they agreed."

"You aren't going to trust them?"

"Of course not. Get the sample in place and when I have hold of the money I'll tell them where it is."

"Why should they trust you?"

"Because they've got me. I shall stay with them until they have the sample. I'm offering myself as insurance. So you see the sooner they get the sample the sooner I can get away. We can give them a similar arrangement for the final deal but first we have to finish this sample business."

"There's no sense in it. It will be the same as before — destabilized. If they think they can culture from it they're wrong."

"I've told them that. Maybe that's what they hope — to get the stuff for 10 per cent — but as long as you are certain that it won't propagate we can't lose, can we? Instead of arguing about it let's give it to them and let them find out for themselves that there is no cheap way. If they want it they will have to pay the price but if they want to keep coming up with 10 per cent for useless samples why should we worry?"

Conway hesitated and then said "Keith. Why would the man Gabriel say he hasn't heard from you? Why would he say he doesn't know where you are?"

"You spoke to him?" Tyler's tone changed again.

"On the number you gave me. For emergencies, you said. In case you didn't get back to me."

Tyler glanced anxiously up and down the street, twisting around in the phone box to look behind him. "Yes, I know we agreed but it wasn't like that. You didn't need to call him."

"How was I supposed to . . ."

"I know, I know. It's all right. Never mind. What did he say, exactly?"

"He said he hadn't heard from you, had no idea where you were. He said he would ask somebody else. He wanted to know where he could contact me."

"You didn't tell him!"

"Of course not. I said I would ring him again. Then I rang off."

Tyler's relief was palpable. "Well, forget it now. It doesn't matter any more. Don't call him back. If they think they can get to you they'll never pay up for the stuff."

"But I still don't understand why he said he hadn't heard from you. He could have said he wasn't at liberty to tell me anything. That would have been understandable at least. But to say he hadn't heard from you — why that?"

"Ralph, it's complicated. Remember, we always expected to be dealing with his backers, the people with the money. Well, we still are, only perhaps he's being left out of things now. You follow me?"

Conway frowned, his small face puckered with concern, his eyes focussed somewhere in the middle of his faded hearthrug. "I see."

"Ralph, as soon as I've seen this sample deal through I'll get back to you. I'll explain everything then, somewhere where we can talk properly."

"How do I get it to you?" Conway's voice was flat, without enthusiasm or even interest, it seemed.

"As we arranged for the main delivery. Use that now."

"But if you won't tell me where you are how can I let you know when it's in place?"

"You can't. We'll have to fix a time. Can you get it there soon? How long will it take you?"

"Delivering it is nothing," Conway said, and he made it sound as if it didn't matter either. "I suppose it would take about two hours."

"Today is out, we have to give them time to get the cash. Tomorrow. Better do it while it's busy — say ten o'clock. Make it ten o'clock tomorrow unless I phone again to say otherwise."

"Yes, all right."

"Ten precisely then." Tyler hoped for more conviction but it was not forthcoming.

"Yes."

"Good man. This is going to work out, you'll see. I'll give you time to get back after the drop then I'll call to confirm receipt, okay?"

"Yes." It sounded mechanical.

"Hang on, Ralph, it's going to be all right." Tyler rang off.

Like so many things desperately awaited, Tyler's phone call, when it came, was an event which seemed to leave things substantially unchanged, and Conway found himself wondering how he had expected to feel. The truth was that he had reached a state of mind in which doubt and dread found an instant niche whereas hope and encouragement had become much harder to establish. He would deliver the sample because he had nothing to lose but, for much the same reason, he knew he would not abandon his plans for the cellar.

In South Africa House Frits de Wet moved between rooms with the quiet urgency of a man determined to stay in control. In the few hours since learning of Tyler's release he had briefed his tiny team, instructed Meester to double Nero's danger money for the third time, restored a 24-hour monitoring régime on Tamala's phone and informed Pretoria of developments by flash coded message. The response, when it came, was lengthy, and originated from the chief of South Africa's intelligence service. It informed de Wet that he had exceeded his authority in approaching the British security service on his own initiative, that the nature and extent of the threat posed by Keith Tyler was to be determined as a matter of urgency and that, to this end, closer collaboration with the British authorities was being pursued at a more senior level. In short: you've made a balls-up but you won't do any more damage because we are taking over now and will attend to you later. At least, that was how de Wet read it.

Chris Collins was sitting through the first half of his double shift when the call from Conway to Tamala was transmitted. It was the reference to Mr Smith that brought him to the edge of his seat because the voice of the caller was totally unfamiliar. The short recording quickly became the centre of intense interest in Jutta's den but it threw no light on the situation other than to prove that someone claiming to be Tyler's close associate did not know that Tyler had been arrested. Tight-lipped, de Wet considered what to do with the information and decided to keep it; in all probability British Special Branch would have picked it up for themselves anyway. In that he was wrong. Conway's call had been overheard by nobody outside South Africa House. Indeed, neither Special Branch nor Randolph's team were operating any phone taps at all. The house where Tyler was being kept was more than adequately wired for sound but telephones were not involved. It was reasoned that Tyler would not use a house phone and Peter Lawson might need the excuse of phoning from outside.

In the plan for phase two the chips were all on Lawson with a back-up which depended on close surveillance and continuous monitoring of conversation within the house. De Wet's team, informed but not invited to participate, was understandably less than happy with the arrangement.

"Everything stacked on one agent! It's crazy." That was Meester.

"They probably reasoned that he would stand a better chance of gaining Tyler's trust that way." Jutta Keiner suggested.

"And if he fails? Then what? Tyler gets free and loses himself in London. We are further back than start."

"He'd better be a good agent, that's all," de Wet muttered.

He would have been dismayed to learn that Peter Lawson was on his first assignment for the British Security Service.

When Tyler got back from the phone booth, Peter Lawson was peeling potatoes.

Tyler looked in the fridge and found a dozen cans of beer and a bottle of wine.

"Who's paying for this?"

"I am so far."

Tyler pulled the tops from two cans and searched for glasses. "Well, I haven't got any money."

"You know what to do about that."

Tyler poured the beer, thinking carefully as he watched the rising froth. "At the meeting we had, just before I got picked up, they said they wanted another sample."

"They still do," Lawson said promptly.

"It was agreed I get 10 per cent, fifty thousand, to show good faith."

"On delivery." Lawson rinsed his potatoes under the tap and scooped up the peelings from the sink. There was no reason to think that he didn't know about it.

"Well," Tyler concluded, "I'm ready to deliver." He watched the man called Peter add a pinch of salt to the water and settle the pan on a high jet before turning round.

"Good," he said. He might have been talking about the dinner. "But there is a condition."

Tyler stiffened. "What condition?"

Lawson picked up his beer glass. "It's very reasonable. When you get handed a suitcase full of money you can see what you've got but when I'm given this precious sample it's not going to mean a damn thing to me, is it?"

"So?"

"So for 24 hours afterwards, or until my employers are satisfied that they've got what they paid for, I keep you on a very short leash."

Tyler began to grin.

"No, it's not much of a condition, is it? But if you try to cut loose with your 10 per cent, my friend, I'll kill you."

Lawson might still have been talking about the potatoes and for a moment Tyler was uncertain how to respond. He just stood there with a half-faded grin and a blankness in his eyes. Then his expression hardened and he coloured slightly. "I've already told your people they can have me as insurance and I was talking about half a million then, not this bloody peanuts. And it works both ways too: how am I supposed to feel safe with fifty thousand in cash once you've got what you want?"

Lawson shrugged. "Bank it, give it to a third party, hide it, do what you like."

The other sniffed and turned away, knowing that he would find it very difficult to do any of those things. The only person he could entrust the money to would be Conway, and he was not prepared to risk it. If he was followed or otherwise caught making any contact with Ralph Conway the show would be over. Tyler was intensely curious about his rescuer. There was something about the man: a supreme self-confidence. He spoke of killing as if it were a routine. Was that possible? Was he a mercenery, ready to work for anybody? Were assassinations included in the service? Was he now armed? Tyler could see no sign of it. All he could see was a man, tall and strong, who busied himself with a frying-pan and a plate of sausage that made his very thoughts seem ridiculous. And yet he had calmly spoken of killing. Well, I too have killed, Tyler told himself, and could do so again if need be. We are two of a kind, you and I, he said to himself with secret pride. We are well matched in this game.

"I've arranged a delivery for ten o'clock tomorrow night," he announced during the uneasy meal "Can you get the money by then?"

"I've told you, I'm ready when you are. Can we do it here?"

"We have to go to collect it."

"Where from?"

"You'll see."

"How big is this thing?"

Tyler looked surprised. "Same as last time."

"I didn't see the last one."

Tyler pointed to a bottle of milk that was still on the table. "About as big as that."

"It's a lot of money for something the size of a milk bottle." Lawson spoke clearly for the sake of the microphones and if Tyler thought it was a silly remark he showed no sign of it.

For those listening it was the first positive indication that Tyler was dealing in something close to his old line of business — a substance rather than a device, at least. Lawson was doing nicely. No reason to move in yet; better to let him follow through. Tyler had obligingly talked himself beyond any possibility of playing the innocent again but, given his head for a bit longer, he could be even more helpful. Keep it up, they said to each other at the receiving end of the microphones. And a mile away, in Stag Place, James Randolph took full responsibility for providing Lawson with fifty thousand pounds in cash.

The sight of 10,000 five-pound notes packed solidly in a cheap attaché case had a powerful effect on Keith Tyler. He counted one neatly squared deck of a thousand pounds and estimated the rest, riffling the little bundles and tossing them in his hands. He held a few notes up to the light and could not suppress his grins and excitement, even with the thought of himself looking like a child at Christmas. Lawson watched him without expression. Collecting the money had involved nothing more than a single telephone call and a trip to a city branch of Barclay's. Had he been followed he would have been seen only to spend a brief time with the assistant manager and to wait his turn for the teller. He had bought the attaché case on the way to the bank.

"Well, what are you going to do with it now you've got it?" It sounded faintly like a challenge.

Tyler smirked. "I'll take my chances. I'm not worried about my side of the deal. You'll want to buy more."

"Not me, my friend."

"As long as you come up with the money I couldn't care less who's buying." Tyler was bubbly and restless for the rest of the afternoon. Lawson spent most of the time with his feet up, reading a paperback.

They left the house just before eight. Lawson backed out the car in which they had arrived and Tyler settled himself in the passenger seat with the attaché case on the floor between his feet. "Make for London Bridge," he said. And that was all he would say about their destination. Before they cleared Ladywell, Tyler had turned to look behind a dozen times. He was still trying to spot a following car on the long straight of the Old Kent Road. Lawson was doing much the same through his rear-view mirror and was impressed by how little there was to see. At least two vehicles were involved and neither was in view long enough to attract attention; after a spell one would fall back and let the other take the lead. They were co-ordinated by radio and there was no need for continuous sight of the quarry; Lawson's car was sending out a very clear signal.

They crossed the bridge in steady traffic though it was only a fraction of the daytime volume. "On to the Monument," Tyler said. "We join the A10 higher up." They passed the end of Cornhill and Threadneedle Street leading to the Bank of England and the heart of the City — deceptively quiet now. Tyler checked his watch for the second time in five minutes but made no comment on their progress.

"How are we doing?" Lawson asked.

"Plenty of time. Just keep going."

They continued along Bishopsgate and through Shoreditch, leaving the city behind and travelling northwards on the main Kingsland Road. It was quite dark now and in the light of the street-lamps Lawson surveyed the derelict buildings and run-down homes that bordered the railway to the right. Where the hell were they going? It was in the Tottenham area that Tyler's anxiety really became noticeable. By then he was regarding his wristwatch as if it were part of the controls. Wherever they were supposed to get to it was evidently important to arrive on time. They were just north of Tottenham, near the intersection with Lordship Lane, when Tyler made what appeared to be a snap decision.

"Stop here," he said suddenly. "Anywhere. Just find a place to park."

Lawson slid neatly into a kerbside space between signs that suggested it would not have been so easy during the day. "Now what?"

"We wait."

Lawson sighed and wound down the window, clearing the reflections from his view of the wing mirror. One car, he was quite certain, had pulled in some way behind. The other one went past a few moments later to stop, no doubt, well in front and out of sight. For a full fifteen minutes they sat there. The monosyllabic conversation revealed nothing to Lawson other than the fact that

Tyler was tense but making a determined effort to stay cool. At exactly five minutes past ten he announced that it was time to move again.

"Where to now?"

"Not far, just go on for a bit."

It seemed that they had scarcely got under way when Tyler again wanted to stop — this time on the car park of the Greyhound Hotel. On its corner site the Greyhound had two separate parking areas linked by a short driveway around the back of the pub. They turned into the south-side parking lot, but had to drive round to the east section to find a vacant place.

"Now what," Lawson demanded as he tugged up the handbrake.

Tyler lifted the case on to his knee and ducked his head to see further through the rear window. A man was walking unsteadily towards a grey Lancia. Another man caught up with him and put an arm round his shoulders for support. He steered him to the car and they took up positions side by side with their elbows on the roof, expressing, it appeared, earnest agreement with one another. Light and shadow alternated on Tyler's face as another vehicle pulled out on to the road. He just kept on peering through the windows.

"Well?"

"This is the place. This is where I collect."

"Not without me, you don't. Unless you leave the money here." Lawson tensed imperceptibly in the half light, not knowing what to expect.

"The money stays with me," Tyler said too quickly. "But there's nothing to stop you coming too," he added.

Lawson climbed out, watching the other closely. He saw him lick his lips and then he said, "Come on then," and Tyler led the way to the men's outside toilet. It was dark there, away from the neon glow of the pub frontage, but a single bulb glowed above the brick cubicle, lighting the entrance. Without hesitating Tyler went past the urinal and pushed open a lavatory door. Still clutching the attaché case he stood on the edge of the lavatory bowl and reached a sinewy arm over the old iron cistern. From a cavity in the brickwork of the wall he produced a metal cylinder rather smaller than the size he had predicted. Tyler stepped down and turned triumphantly. His fish-cold eyes seemed to gleam with their own light as he thrust the object into Lawson's hands.

"There you are. Now let's get out of here."

Lawson swore silently and slipped the cylinder out of sight under his jacket. "How long has it been there?"

Tyler smirked and made a show of checking the time. "Nine minutes," he said confidently and he guessed, correctly, that at that moment Ralph Conway would be driving carefully northwards on the A10.

As they walked back across the parking lot the two car-leaners were still there but conversation had been abandoned. One of them was standing with both hands on the rear bumper — vomiting.

NINE

At ten a.m. on the day following Conway's phone call to Gabriel Tamala a motor cyclist threaded his way skilfully through the traffic of Bayswater Road and puttered into Kensington Palace Gardens. He throttled back alongside a high wall set with iron spikes and barbed wire and turned smoothly into the gate of number thirteen. His arrival was watched routinely on closed circuit television as he propped the bike, removed his skid-lid and stepped confidently between the ornate carriage lamps to the heavy oak doors. One door swung open and he entered the fortress that is the Embassy of the USSR in London.

Max Cullen knew London very well. He had lived there for most of his 31 years and, among other things, had worked as a courier. Politically he was far left but not actively so. He had a flair for languages and had once completed Linguaphone courses in Russian and German; he lacked the self-discipline for formal study and recognized exams. He had been to Russia twice but would have laughed at the suggestion that he was a Russian agent or a spy. He passed on no secrets because he knew none; he had no access to classified information of any sort. Still, he would have had to admit that he had occasionally been helpful to the régime in small ways and had been rewarded by the special treatment he had received during his second tourist trip to the Soviet Union. He had since been called upon to run little errands, or follow someone or act as unofficial guide for certain people who called at the Aeroflot offices where he now worked. Nor could he have denied that the extra attention he had received in Moscow had included a little informal training in such duties.

While he was no stranger to the embassy in London, Cullen had never really got to know any of the staff because he did not move in the same social circles. Whenever there had been communication on some little business matter it had been handled by the same two or three people who were rather stiff and unfriendly. Only one of them was left now; the others had gone following the defection of Oleg Gordiyevsky in September 1985. The one who was left appeared in response to a buzz from the reception desk when Cullen presented himself. He was a middle-aged, dyspeptic man with wispy fair hair.

Comrade Ulyanov was an accredited diplomat, though not a very senior one, and his position with the KGB was even less exalted. But Ulyanov was a survivor. He did his work carefully and thoroughly, just as he was told. What he lacked in talent he tried to make up for in diligence and loyalty — loyalty to the *Komitet*, his country, his masters and everyone and everything that might have a bearing on his continued employment in comfortable western duty stations. Why he was not expelled along with the 31 others in the embassy's own black September is a matter for conjecture, because his name must certainly have been on the list. The most likely explanation is that he was thought to be relatively harmless and was allowed to stay in the hope that he would become useful as a sort of tag who would identify, by association, the new team which would gradually replace the ousted one.

He greeted Cullen with a perfunctory handshake and a few words which served to satisfy the front office that Cullen could be admitted a little further into the expensive little enclave of Soviet territory. After signing him in, Ulyanov then led Cullen, still clutching his crash-helmet, to an interview room conveniently located on the ground floor near the front of the building. They sat down òn dining-room chairs at a mahogany table. There was a print of a portrait of Lenin high on the wall and a standard lamp beneath it. Otherwise the room was without decoration or furnishings. There was no reading material.

"We will not keep you long," Ulyanov said into the silence.

Cullen didn't much care. He placed his helmet on the floor beside his chair, thrust his hands in his pockets, crossed his outstretched legs and just sat back. But Ulyanov was right and after a few minutes they were joined by a man whom Cullen had never seen before. He looked a little younger than Ulyanov and was clearly his senior. He was introduced, deferentially, as Comrade Zinyakin. Cullen studied him with mixed feelings. Here was a man who must surely carry more weight than the characters he normally dealt with. Here was a man who could possibly authorize better perks for helpful people; the state airline having been disappointing in that respect. Unfortunately it was not the best time to meet such a person. Lately there had been few opportunities for earning merit and the most recent job he had been entrusted with had gone badly. Zinyakin came straight to the point, as if he had no time to waste.

"Mr Cullen, you have been to Moscow, yes?"

"Yeah, twice."

"And you know London very well, it is your, er, home town, I think."

"Well, more or less. I was born . . ."

"You said you knew London like the back of your own hand."

"I know the old town pretty well."

"And you told us that if ever we needed a man who knew his way around we could depend on you, yes?"

Cullen resented the obvious line of questioning. "Look, if it's the last job you're getting at, I told Alex what happened. It wasn't my fault. It was nothin' to do with knowing your way around. I didn't get bloody lost."

Zinyakin was a restless man whose dark eyes had a feverish glow and were never still. He seemed to be impatient with everything he said and did, as if he always wanted to be doing or saying something else. Certainly he had more than enough on his plate at that time and far more than his official position might suggest. He was also an accredited diplomat but with responsibility to the cultural attaché. This fairly low position in the hierarchy permitted him to move about quite freely and without formality. But his real job was to restructure the London network which Gordiyevsky's defection had wrecked. His usual position was deputy sectional head in the KGB's First Chief Directorate.

"You did not get lost. Good. That is something at least. But what I would like to know is why you lost the man you were following. I understand he was about two metres tall and had bright red hair."

"He wasn't anywhere near that tall but it wouldn't have made any difference. The way it happened I didn't 'ave a chance."

"Tell me exactly."

Cullen felt like saying "get stuffed". He'd done his best for them and now they talked as if they owned him. But he took a deep breath and started to explain. "I'd followed him half-way round the Underground. He was obviously expecting to be followed."

"Did he see you?"

"Nah, I'm certain of it."

"Go on."

"Well, he decided to leave the tube at Tottenham Court Road. He went up the escalator still walking, two steps at a time. I was behind him, not too close but well-placed. He'd just got off the top when this woman collapsed in front of me."

"Collapsed?"

"Well, fell down. Fainted or tripped or something. I couldn't see, she was a bit in front. Anyway they stopped the escalator and there was a sort of scrum while they got her up and out the way."

"Then?"

"Well, it slowed me up, see. I saw the redhead go out but when I got to the street he'd vanished. I reckoned he'd jumped on a bus 'cause there was one just moving off. I tried to catch up but I couldn't. By the time I got a taxi and checked out the bus he'd gone. It had been through another stop by then so he could have got off. I didn't have a chance did I?"

"The woman who fell, had you seen her before?"

"Don't think so. I only got a quick look as I ran past but it was nobody I know."

"About what age was she?"

"Hard to say. I only got a quick look. Not all that old, forties, maybe."

"Not a tottering old woman then."

"Oh no, she wasn't an old dodderer."

For several seconds, a long period of composure for Zinyakin, he maintained a scathing expression but said nothing, as if he were giving the youngster a chance to draw his own conclusions. But Cullen only blinked.

Then Zinyakin turned to Ulyanov who had kept a neutral silence. "Unless you wish to say anything I don't think we need to keep Mr Cullen from his work any longer."

"Of course," Ulyanov said immediately, and sprang to his feet to show Cullen out. Zinyakin nodded a farewell, murmured something and left the room.

Zinyakin's assignment could be extended indefinitely, but he was expected to get a new intelligence-gathering network up and running as quickly as possible. It was anticipated that he would be recalled to Moscow Centre as soon as that point was reached. Already more than a score of well-placed agents with and without legal cover had been slipped in place at Zinyakin's instruction. These were now assisting in the recruitment and administration of a full-scale organization based on British nationals. The KGB chief was anxious to avoid contact between his new net and the remnants of the old one; the possibility that Britain had deliberately left a few blown agents in place as 'indicators' had not been overlooked. As soon as the new net was fully operational these doubtful elements would be withdrawn but, in the meantime, and to Zinyakin's irritation, they had to occupy key positions in several ongoing projects. For a while he was tempted to have Ulyanov recalled there and then, and to sever all connections with the remains of his so-called team in the field, but he realized that he was not ready for it. What had to be done next was not just intelligence gathering. It could lead to direct action on British soil. Better, in a way, to use those who were already on the skids than to risk losing clean, new agents if things went wrong. Zinyakin made up his mind and rang for Ulyanov.

"Well, comrade," he said brusquely. "What do you think?"

Ulyanov dithered. "It is possible, I suppose, that the boy was delayed not by accident. I think we can believe his story, about the woman falling in front of him."

"Of course we can. So let us suppose that the woman was protecting Smith. Why would she do that? Who would gain?"

"Smith himself could have arranged . . ."

"She may have been Smith's accomplice, yes, that is one possibility. There are others are there not?"

Ulyanov swallowed. Whichever way he looked at it the implications were bad. If the woman was not Smith's accomplice then the truth was inescapable: Smith had been under surveillance.

Unhappily, Ulyanov said as much and Zinyakin seemed gratified, as if he had scored a point.

But Zinyakin was not content to leave it there. "We know nothing," he said, "of this man Smith. It could be that he is well known to the British police or other authorities. The first we heard of him was when he approached the Free Africa Movement. Perhaps they were careless or maybe we are not the only ones they have contacted."

Zinyakin's next move was to send an urgent message to Moscow. Despite his seniority in HQ, there was very little that he could actually initiate without prior approval. All agents abroad were in the same boat and there was almost nothing they could do about it. It had been decided, decades before, that to minimize damage by defectors and to strengthen Moscow's central control at the same time, all case files, records of meetings, recruitments, payments made, photographs etc., should be regularly transferred to the vast data banks of Moscow Centre. Consequently, at any one time, there was surprisingly little on record in the residencies and if an officer wanted to check back more than three months or so he was obliged to do so through Moscow. It was a system designed for maximum security and all other considerations were secondary. The inefficiency, together with the frustrations and delays forced upon field officers was considered to be unavoidable. In any case, initiative at the personal level was not to be encouraged. So Zinyakin sent off his request, Moscow duly processed it and two days later Ulyanov received his orders: with the co-operation of Gabriel Tamala he was to carry out a full security sweep of the FAM in London.

While Zinyakin was waiting for Moscow's green light and details of the previous security sweeps of the FAM, the head of the South African intelligence service was ordering lunch in a Knightsbridge club. Doctor Constand Bronkhorst was the guest of Sir Reginald Farren of the British Ministry of Defence.

"Not quite as good as it used to be, here," Sir Reginald told the Afrikaner over an avocado salad. "But I don't know anywhere better on occasions like this."

The other nodded approvingly, his eyes on a rack of lamb. He was a small, thin-faced man with a neatly trimmed beard and an inexplicable appetite.

"But you didn't come over to London just for a decent lunch, Connie. Why the surprise visit?"

Bronkhorst touched his lips with his napkin before speaking. "Nothing very special. I was due to come next month but brought it forward, that's all. I have a few messages for you but nothing earth-shattering."

"Good. I was afraid something ominous was in the wind; thought perhaps the mine had collapsed." Farren seemed relieved but not entirely satisfied. The two had known each other for many years and it was not like Connie to arrive unexpectedly and change the routine of their regular meetings. There had to be a reason and he was very curious to know what it was.

In South Africa the military and other security and intelligence services routinely work together on both internal and external operations. Internal threats to South Africa commonly have immediate military potential in the form of insurgency or guerilla activity. As in Belfast, collaboration between the state's protective agencies is both close and constant. In his younger days Connie Bronkhorst had commanded a minesweeper and later joined naval intelligence. He now included among his close associates virtually all the top brass of the South African security machine.

With three thousand miles of coastline and a comparable stretch of land border with less than friendly neighbours, the guardians of South Africa need the very best in communications intelligence. They have it in a top secret establishment about ten kilometres from the Simonstown naval base near Cape Town. There, built into the side of a mountain, is a three storey control centre for a communications and intelligence system which can spy and eavesdrop on everything from Soviet ships in the Indian Ocean to SWAPO guerilla units in Angola. The centre is called Silvermine and it is in no danger of collapsing.

In 1957 the British government under Prime Minister Harold Wilson terminated a twenty-year-old agreement by which the Royal Navy could use the Simonstown naval base. It was done for political reasons, of course, to demonstrate to the world that Britain was not prepared to maintain defence agreements with the racist régime in Pretoria. This did not prevent the exchange of intelligence between the secret services; there are no political points to be scored by abandoning secret practices. Because of Silvermine the flow of information tends to be in Britain's (and NATO's) favour. This puts South Africa's caretakers in a strong position for negotiating with their British counterparts. Connie Bronkhorst was always very confident when he wanted a small favour.

"I must admit," he said, sitting back after his meal and fondling a bulbous glass, "that only the French can make good brandy. Some of our wines are as good as anybody's but the brandy . . ." He shook his head. "It must be something in the Charente soil."

Farren looked at his watch. "I must be getting back, Connie. Got one or two things on this afternoon."

"Of course, of course." He drained the last drops and suddenly became businesslike. "So. I shall see you tomorrow morning then at half-past nine, usual place."

"That's as quick as I can make it, I'm afraid. If you'd given me warning I could have changed the programme a bit, but these chaps are all organized for this afternoon; can't put 'em off now."

"No problem, Reggie, I have plenty to do myself on this trip." He produced a tiny note-book and checked over what looked like a shopping list — which indeed it partly was. "Oh, there is one thing you might do for me." He had not just remembered it, nor was it on his list.

"Here it comes," Farren told himself.

"Yes, I wonder if you will be seeing your friend Kingsley this afternoon."

"He'll be there tomorrow, you can see him yourself."

Bronkhorst smiled. "You know him much better than I do." He had had only formal contacts with the head of MI5. "I would be grateful if you would pass on a message for me."

"Oh, well, certainly."

"It would be appreciated. I understand his people are handling a little matter which is really our concern. In fact, they could be said to be handling it for us."

"Glad to be of service." Farren said cautiously.

"The trouble is, Reggie, that we are giving it A1 priority and there is concern that the operational levels are not getting the proper feedback. In fact, I don't recall seeing them so upset for a long time. It is really threatening to, er, sour things between us out of all proportion and that would be a pity."

"First I've heard of it."

"Well it's a very small operation and that's one reason why I'm asking if you can use your good influence. I would prefer not to make a more formal approach."

"I'll certainly have a word, Connie. For all our differences there are bigger things at stake than domestic squabbles. I'll see what I can do to pour the proverbial oil." And with that assurance Sir Reginald Farren went off to his meeting still curious but full of good intentions.

It was past midnight when Peter Lawson left Tyler at the house and set off alone to deliver the steel cylinder. Had Tyler been able to follow him he would have seen only that Lawson drove to an all-night transport cafe on the A21 and arrived within half a minute of two other cars which parked, one on either side of him. A thoroughly undistinguished-looking man then came across and slipped into the passenger seat beside him. Another nondescript, from the other side, climbed in behind. Lawson produced the cylinder, holding it carefully at the top with the tips of his fingers. "It might have been smudged under my coat but it hasn't been handled much," he said.

The Special Branch man beside him held open a polythene bag and stared at the object as if he had never seen such a thing. "Do you know what it is?"

"No, but he seemed certain that it's safe to handle and that's the main thing. I couldn't show too much ignorance. We'll know soon enough."

"I hope so." The SB man sealed the bag and half turned to his partner who was leaning over the seat for a better view. "Any ideas Jeff?"

"Not a bloody clue. Looks like just a container; could be anything inside. Not ticking is it?" They both grinned — a soundless show of teeth in the half light. "Pity we didn't get the bugger who delivered it."

"Not entirely stupid, our friend Tyler," Lawson remarked as he moved to get out. "I must get back and see if he's tucked up in bed."

"Well he won't have got lost, that's for bloody sure. We've got surveillance on that house as tight as a nun's knees."

Lawson closed the door and slapped the car roof in a parting farewell.

The only fingerprints on the cylinder proved to be those of Tyler and Lawson. Special Branch could tell, almost at a glance, that it was not explosive and they were relieved to confirm, after chasing around for equipment at two in the morning, that it was not radio-active either. Daintry himself stayed up to see it dismantled. "It's just a length of galvanized pipe," he muttered as he tried to twist one end and then the other. It was two inches in diameter and about eight inches long, threaded and capped at both ends. "Must have been tightened up in a vice, though. I can't budge it." Two others tried with no more success. "Haven't we got a couple of pipe wrenches downstairs?" The driver who had escorted it to Special Branch HQ was already on his way to get them.

Daintry watched while the driver, who was also a mechanic, laid the cylinder across a telephone directory on the floor and gripped the middle of the pipe with one wrench. Daintry took the other one and adjusted it to fit the cap which projected beyond the directory. With the driver standing on his wrench, and Daintry thrusting down on his, the cap suddenly turned and Daintry slammed his little finger between the wrench handle and the floor. He swore and shook his hand about while the driver picked up the cylinder and continued to unscrew it.

Over a cleared table they watched intently while the cap was removed to reveal a neat disc of styrofoam. Using a paper-knife as a lever Daintry prised out the styrofoam and began to pull it slowly, like a piston, from its cylinder. It was in two sections held together with Scotch tape and Daintry knew then what to expect next. He waited impatiently while they dusted once more for finger-prints (there were none) and then began to unwind the tape. To those watching it seemed to take an age but eventually the two halves lay apart and snugly buried in one of them was a small glass phial. Inside were a few millilitres of what looked like cloudy water.

"Don't touch the bottle," Daintry barked. "We've seen as much as we can make sense of." And still nursing his little finger he went to make a phone call.

Commander Daintry and James Randolph were at once agreed on where the sample could be sent for analysis. The Home Office forensic laboratories with their various specializations, could cope with most things, but there was only one destination for material believed to be so dangerous as to have military value. It would have to be taken to an establishment located in rural Wiltshire, a few miles north of Salisbury. There, with the sort of security that only the Ministry of Defence can operate, is the military research and development centre of Porton Down. Randolph offered to arrange it.

Sir Reginald Farren was in the bathroom when the call came through. His wife shouted through the door. "Reggie, Richard Kingsley's on the phone. Reggie?"

"Coming, coming." He was in the habit of listening to the seven o'clock news while he washed and shaved. He turned off a soap-spattered transistor which was perched among his wife's shampoos and came out wearing a towel.

"Hello, Richard."

"Ah, Reggie. Hope I haven't caught you at a bad time." Kingsley's voice had an unmistakable piping tone.

"Not at all."

"Good, well, apropos of what we spoke about yesterday, there's been a development."

"Oh, really?"

"Yes, well, we have a little specimen that we'd like the boffins to look at for us. Your PD chaps would probably be able to make most sense of it, but we do need it done in a hurry, you understand."

"Where is it now?"

"Safely under lock and key but we want to send it straight down there this morning. I'm calling to ask if you can prime them for us. I'll give you all the details later of course. Just want to be sure that there won't be a hitch."

"I'll get priority on it and confirm with you later. You'll be at the meeting this morning won't you?"

"Oh yes, this business won't interfere with my schedule. I'm just anxious to get the thing teed up that's all. As I explained yesterday we want it over and done with."

"Absolutely. And, er, you will smooth the ruffled feathers, won't you? Perhaps you could speak to Connie yourself. We'll be seeing him later."

"He ought to be pleased with the progress," Kingsley intoned. "I'll certainly have a word."

In 1975 a convention banning the possession, production and use of biological weapons was ratified by Great Britain, the USA and the Soviet Union. Three years later unconfirmed reports, reaching the western press via Brussels, described spy satellite photographs of fermentation vats in Soviet military installations. Specially designed tanker wagons were also said to have been photographed on railway lines leading to the facilities. In 1981 reports appeared in the western newspapers of biological as well as chemical weapons having been used in Laos, Cambodia and Afghanistan. It was intelligence of this sort, studied in the original at NATO headquarters, which persuaded the British government to broaden the scope of defensive research at Porton Down. By 1985 it was staffed and equipped for research into the nature and control of disease organisms as well as chemical weapons.

Using a scanning electron microscope it took Doctor Mary Turnbull only minutes to determine that the cloudy liquid in the specimen tube was a virus culture. Because of certain structural characteristics she was also prepared to speculate a little. "Definitely a virus," she announced confidently. "Not exactly like anything I'm familiar with but I'd guess it's an animal virus — not one that affects plants or bacteria. We shall have to assume that it affects humans."

James Randolph, who had been permitted to accompany her to the lab, nodded slowly. "How can you find out more?"

"Well not by looking, I'm afraid. We have to set up a series of trials now to see what it can do to human tissues in culture."

"How long will that take?"

"It depends how much you need to know. We ought to be able to discover which parts of the body it affects within a day or two but we still won't know much about its military potential."

126

"How could you get that sort of information?"

"We can't really. The best we can do is to study factors such as virulence and transmission in experimental animals. But, of course the problem doesn't normally arise. We are concerned with defence measures, usually. Our job is to find out how best to prepare for the worst imaginable scenarios." The woman was in her forties and still, literally, in very good shape. Randolph found her attractive in an impersonal sort of way.

"We haven't time for much research," he said. "But I would be extremely grateful if you could identify the virus and then let me have a list of all the laboratories in the UK which might be working with such a thing."

"Oh, I can do that," she said at once. "It won't be a very long list."

"You are being very helpful," Randolph murmured. And then, as she was escorting him out as far as the first security check, he said, "As to the military potential, perhaps I can give you a clue: whatever this thing is it seems to be particularly interesting to certain people who are fighting the régime in South Africa."

TEN

COMRADE ULYANOV WAS relieved that Gabriel Tamala was being co-operative. It made things simpler and that made for an easy, straightforward report with full marks for diplomacy. It wasn't much of a job, checking out the tin-pot little headquarters and asking a few obvious questions, but it could be written up into a good report. There was also opportunity for offering guidance and showing thoroughness in the task. Some might do half a job and feel satisfied but not Vladimir Ulyanov; he would be most diligent. He could be relied upon. That was why he had been chosen. Ulyanov knew his own security drill backwards and was never careless in the daily routine. He invariably shredded departmental memos on classified subjects. He never failed to check the page numbering of loose-leaved files and was never careless on the telephone. Vladimir Ulyanov's conduct was exemplary.

His companion and driver that morning was a morose character called Vlasov who was with the Scientific and Technical Division. There were S & T men in every residency and they were regarded, by those closer to the policy-makers, as being slightly inferior but absolutely indispensable beings, like plumbers. Vlasov knew where they were going and what he had to do but he was piqued at having been summarily instructed to assist Ulyanov; in his opinion it should have been the other way round.

Tamala was expecting them but had given an assurance that his staff would not be forewarned. Not that they knew anything about the Smith project; on that subject he had confided in nobody. From the very first he had handled it personally and nothing had been put in writing. If Smith's disappearance was the result of some indiscretion then Smith himself was probably to blame. But by all means come and do a sweep, he had said readily. We have nothing to hide from our friends, or if we have, I would like to know about it.

They parked outside the converted North London shop and went straight in. There was nothing clandestine about the visit. It was simply a case of an overtly friendly government performing a service for a struggling political group. Tamala greeted them, ushered them inside and assembled his staff. The movement supported only four people on the permanent payroll at the London headquarters: Tamala himself, a girl secretary, a bearded bull of a man, and one privately described by Ulyanov as "that strutting little peacock, Nero."

Ulyanov began to address them in heavily accented English while Vlasov, without comment, opened the first of two leather cases which he had carried in with him from the car. Ignoring the group, though all eyes were upon him, Vlasov then donned headphones and produced a compact electronic unit about the size of a cassette recorder. He switched on, activated the sensors and began, slowly and methodically to quarter the room.

Ulyanov's words might have been the grunts and groans of a distant farmyard for all they affected Nero Boko. His normally active brain was paralysed by the terrible fascination of what he was seeing. He knew nothing of electronic detection. He could only guess what the headphones might convey and could only hope that somehow they would fail. In the few seconds between the Russians' arrival and his being summoned before them he had managed to pluck the wall bug from its nest under the light-switch and had pressed the deactivating button so hard that his thumb bore the imprint. He pressed it still, in his pocket, for he was afraid to let go. But it was the phone bug that really threatened disaster because it was still inside the phone on Tamala's desk. Nero began to sweat even as he struggled to keep calm and think of a way out. He knew that any attempt to leave at that point would be as good as a confession. *Think, think*! But it was just a word, a kind of noise, a tiny echo somewhere between his thudding temples. Nothing connected. Nothing would respond. The bearded one, whose name was Ben, caught his eye and grimaced at something Ulyanov had said. Nero tried to grin in reply and he was conscious of the tightness in the muscles of his face. Ben continued to stare at him and Nero turned away. His hands were shaking.

When Ulyanov had finished the room he moved through the dingy corridor and into the outer office. Tamala's own office would come last. Ulyanov shifted with the group to gather round one of the filing cabinets. Tamala said something then snapped his fingers and Nero suddenly realized that he was the centre of attention. He stared back woodenly until the word 'keys' finally penetrated. Hurriedly, he snatched the keys from a desk and handed them over. Ulyanov smirked with satisfaction and began to lecture them on the most elementary and obvious rule of security: whoever is responsible for keys should never leave them lying about. They should be kept on the person and handed directly to whoever else is to be responsible during one's absence. Nero heard none of it. He was conscious only of the sound of Vlasov's movements from the next room.

Tamala's sanctum was quite small but, being at the rear of the building, it was furthest from the traffic noise and suffered the least disturbance generally. When Vlasov got there he paused in the doorway and made some adjustment to the detector. Then he began passing it over the walls, floor, furniture and fittings as systematically as could be managed. It took several minutes and at the end of it he removed the headphones, folded the unit back into its case and returned to where he had left the other piece of equipment. He was now able to say with complete confidence that there was nothing hidden on the premises which was operating off its own power. No miniature transmitter, however well-concealed, could have escaped him. By that time Ulyanov and the others were trooping through the corridor and Vlasov had to stand back for a moment to let them pass. But again he kept his face averted and if Nero searched there for hope he found nothing.

Vlasov's other case opened to reveal a keyboard unit in the bottom half and a digital display screen in the lid. He switched on, pressed a combination of keys and watched the display confirm that everything was in order. Then he took the open case over to the telephone and inserted a phono-jack into a port on the side of the machine. At the other end was a special terminal by which he made a connection between the telephone and the test kit. He dialled a number in the ordinary way and watched the display while he listened to the ringing tone. When the call was answered Vlasov identified himself and said "hold for testing". In quick succession he pressed several keys then paused until the test results appeared on the two-line, 80-character display. He did this no less than six times and when he had finished he knew that that line was free not only of bugs but of wire taps, tape recorders and even induction taps — by which conversations can be picked up without anything actually touching the wire. Tamala's own phone was on a separate line and when he went to test it Ulyanov and the others were already in the room.

There was no need for Vlasov to unscrew the mouthpiece from the handset. Its tiny secret was detected and identified instantly. He felt a surge of excitement but had the presence of mind not to show it. Instead he stole a glance at those who were watching. They were not paying much attention to Ulyanov. It was in that one glance that Vlasov recognized the fear in Nero's eyes but, for the sake of appearance, and also for thoroughness, he continued with the test routine and pretended that he was having difficulty because of Ulyanov's voice. Obligingly, Ulyanov led the group away until the technician had finished. It took very little time for Vlasov to remove the bug and before he left he found an equally brief opportunity to whisper the vital words to Gabriel Tamala.

Ulyanov never forgave the S & T man for what he did next. On the way back to the embassy Vlasov said nothing about the bug in his pocket. He would not reply directly when he was asked whether the sweep had turned anything up. Instead he made the very most of upstaging Ulyanov when it came to debriefing with Comrade Zinyakin.

"I have to report, comrade," he said, "that Tamala's telephone had been fitted with a transmitting device." And he presented the said object, now nestled on cotton wool in a matchbox, for inspection by his senior while Ulyanov could only gape.

Zinyakin examined the tiny disc with the threadlike wires but was obviously none the wiser for it. Vlasov coughed and told him that it was of American manufacture.

"American!"

"Yes, comrade. But such things are easily obtained and I could not expect the CIA or the British to use that type of thing in this instance."

"Then who?"

"I can only say, comrade, that it would be someone acting illegally here, even without the knowledge of the British." The inference was obvious but Vlasov wisely left it for his master to state it.

"The South Africans themselves."

Vlasov's deferential nod said *if you say so, sir.*

"This is an inferior device, is that what you are saying?" Zinyakin probed.

"Not inferior. It is an excellent choice if you need something that is quick and easy to connect and will run indefinitely. This model runs off the very small telephone current. There is no battery. But, of course, it can be found. Now, if you have the co-operation of the telephone authorities you can tap the line in such a way that . . ."

Zinyakin waved a hand: "I know that."

"Yes, comrade. And even without official co-operation it is possible to tap the wires but it needs some technical knowledge and the units are . . ."

Again Zinyakin cut him short. "You have made your point: this thing was put there by somebody who had little time and no knowledge — probably working for the South Africans. The question now is whether he came from outside or whether he is on the inside."

At this point Vlasov began to choose his words very carefully indeed. "Er, when I was doing the tests, comrade, the others were all present. Only Tamala had known we were coming. One of the others, they call him Nero, was looking very worried. Also, Tamala told comrade Ulyanov that there had been no evidence of any break-in or other interference with the office."

"If the guilty one was there then he must have known that you would find the thing."

"Certainly, comrade." The moment was right and Vlasov seized it. "For that reason I had to tell Tamala what had occurred."

Ulyanov almost choked but his protests died in his throat at the sight of Zinyakin's face. The latter paused only for a moment and then said, "I can see that you were forced to decide. If you had said nothing the traitor would have been given time to escape. If you were mistaken and he is not the traitor then nothing is lost. You made the right decision."

Vlasov tried not to show his elation but when they left the room he and Ulyanov parted without a word.

James Randolph rotated the photographs he was holding and stared at them hopelessly while Mary Turnbull walked briskly away to bring more. He was sitting in an easy chair in a little annexe to her laboratory which she used as a private retreat. On a crowded table there was a tea maker, family photographs, a box of tissues, a handbag — this last being used as a paperweight on a pile of data printouts — and an assortment of those odds and ends which simply don't accumulate in communal places.

"That's the best one," she told him when she got back. "But these show some very interesting features."

He smiled at her, rather wanly. "You'll have to interpret," he said. "It means nothing at all to me."

"Oh, of course, Force of habit," she explained. "Normally we can only talk about our work here among ourselves so whenever I talk shop it's to people who are already steeped in it."

He was standing now and she stood beside him and took hold of the edge of the electron micrograph. Her fingers were clinically clean and at that distance he was aware of the faint fragrance of a perfume that was anything but clinical. He found it all very difficult to reconcile with the check-points and armed guards that he had negotiated only minutes before.

"This is a virus particle, what we call a virion." She traced its outline with her little finger. "And this is the membrane of a cell that is being penetrated. Notice these thin strands; these are the processes of rather spidery cells called melanocytes. Now, on this other photograph you can see how the virus is in contact with one of these strands. It seems to be the invasion route because in every instance that we have seen there is an association between the virus and one or more of these strands." She shuffled the pack and extracted another arcane study in light and shade. "On this one we have quite a different picture. Here the virus is actually multiplying and it's in a nerve cell. These paler clusters are the new viruses but there appears to be more variation than I would expect. It's as if the strain is unstable and doesn't remain true to type."

"We have reason to believe that it was made that way deliberately." Randolph said, and his expression told her that he would say no more.

"Oh, I see." She looked puzzled for a moment but then went on. "You must understand that I'm trying to draw conclusions from the very first indications. Nothing is certain but it *looks* as if your virus is essentially neurotropic — that is living and multiplying in nerve cells — but is able to invade the body through the skin by associating with the melanocytes. It may be significant that in the human embryo the melanocytes come from material that later forms the nervous system. It may also be significant that . . ."

Randolph heard her out in silence and when she had finished he said, "I may have to ask you to come and explain all this to certain other people but in the meantime I would be grateful if you could educate me in the basics of this business. I mean, I'm not sure I know what a virus is."

She surprised him then by saying "neither am I", but she went on to explain. "They are unique, you see. Some people still argue that they are not living things at all. You'll probably find that the dictionary avoids the issue and just calls them 'infective agents'. They can only grow inside the cells of things that are living. Essentially they are packets of genetic material. The packet itself is made of protein. One way or another they get the genetic core into a live host cell where it uses the cell's resources to build new viruses. They are all very small, of course. You could fit hundreds of millions on a pinhead."

She led him through to a lift as they talked. She pressed a button on the unmarked panel which took them down, Randolph guessed, about the equivalent of three floors.

Reading his thoughts she said "I understand it is bomb-proof."

He nodded and asked, "Are there any other viruses which can penetrate the skin?"

"A few, but not dangerous types and certainly not nerve viruses. Well not yet anyway," she added. "New strains are turning up all the time."

"Then how would the other known nerve viruses infect us?" Randolph was not aware of the reduced pressure as they stepped out of the lift into the deep laboratory but a system of pumps and compressors ensured that air from the lab would not be carried up by the lift. Not that the air was anything but pure, but even in the best establishments accidents might happen once in a million years, so the low pressure was an extra precaution. That once could be tomorrow.

"It varies," she said. "Rabies, for example, has to be injected by a bite from the infected animal. Polio virus can invade through the thin membrances of the mouth and throat if you breathe infected droplets, but they seem harmless compared with this." She turned and looked at him squarely. "It can't be natural, but I suppose you know that, don't you?"

"What do you mean?"

"I mean it's just so far removed from any known form that I don't believe it can have arisen spontaneously. It's been created, deliberately developed. Its special properties may have been a chance occurrence but probably even that was caused by tinkering."

"We assumed there would be a human hand behind it. Have you any suggestions?"

She shook her head. "I have the list ready for you but I can tell you that none will be working routinely on anything like this."

"Then we shall just have to check them all."

She led him to a glass and stainless-steel chamber that looked cosmic rather than subterranean, but it was not difficult to work out that some of the complicated gadgetry was for remote manipulation of the little glass containers which were arranged in numbered rows inside.

"These are your cultures," she said. "We've been working a 24 hour schedule on them with hourly sequences. The tissues are grown on glass slips and to withdraw them for study we pass them through here." She indicated a tubular structure projecting from the inner wall. "That sterilizes them and makes them safe to handle."

He looked away, feeling claustrophobic. "There isn't much space down here."

A bearded man in a white lab coat emerged from the lift and stared at them as he went over to another chamber. Strangers in the vault were rare.

"It's big enough," she said. "We don't spend much time here. Most of the real work gets done above."

"Why do you think this thing would be so deadly?" he asked on the way up.

She hesitated. "Look, you must understand that these are just indications from tissue cultures, but even so I have never seen a nerve virus destroy cells so rapidly. If it travels through to the central nervous system at that rate it would be horrific."

"And the method of transmission would be unique, you say."

"Again, I can only tell you how it looks. Human skin is not easily breached by viruses but the penetration rate in these cultures was spectacular. If it's that invasive in the free state it will certainly be unique." She shook her head as if to get rid of the thought. "Devastating."

In her den he looked once more at the electron micrograph before packing the prints away in a manilla folder.

"Now let me get this quite clear," he said finally. "These cells with the threads coming from them, the melanocytes, they occur in the skin of all human beings and many other animals but they are not always very active, is that right?"

"In general terms, yes."

"And their function is to produce skin pigment."

"Yes."

"But it's only the relatively dormant ones that this virus can make use of. The very active cells don't get invaded."

"That's what we found."

Randolph shook his head incredulously. "The world's first racially discriminating germ weapon and it has to turn up in England."

"Perhaps it's just as well that it has," she said quietly. "You are here to stop it. You must stop it."

"We will," Randolph said grimly. "One way or another."

Frits de Wet could only guess at the manoeuvres which had brought about the new co-operation. Somebody up top had used his weight and the pressure waves had evidently reached the inscrutable little Anglo with the electric blue eyes. Otherwise he would have kept the bombshell to himself. And it was a bombshell.

"At least you must agree that we didn't overreact. Christ, man, this is as bad as anything we could have imagined. There are lunatics in the FAM who would not hesitate to spread the thing around if they got hold of it. It wouldn't just be our problem, either. If all it needs is contact between white skins it could cause a pandemic in the West that would make AIDS look like a joke."

Randolph did not deny it.

"And Moscow Centre are in this up to their armpits, I tell you."

Randolph agreed with that as well but he was not so sure of their motives and he said so.

De Wet frowned. "What do you mean by that?"

"I mean that the man who was negotiating on behalf of the FAM was Russian, certainly. But in my experience the Russians do not pay for military gains that they can't subsequently control. If Moscow acquired this I would not expect them to hand it over to the FAM to let loose."

"Listen, man, Moscow is orchestrating the activities of the FAM in my country. They'd *supervise* the job for them."

"If and when they wanted it used, yes, I think they would supervise it. But their immediate concern is to secure it, to have control. As far as we know it is unique and its true potential can only be guessed. Now that probably disturbs Moscow as much as it worries us. They want it because they don't want anyone else to have it. They will work on it and assess for themselves its military potential. The important thing for them now is to secure that option. Very probably it would never be used."

De Wet clicked his tongue with impatience. "You're splitting hairs. The threat is there and the risk is obvious. To hell with probabilities. There is no such thing as a safe risk."

"You misunderstand me," Randolph said calmly. "I am only stating the position as I see it. I'm not questioning the fact that it must be stopped."

"Good. So what do we do about it?"

Wincing inwardly at the 'we' Randolph said, "I don't see any reason to change course. I have full confidence in our agent, and Special Branch have an extremely tight net around the two of them."

"But what the hell are we waiting for? You have all you need and more. Jump on the bastard."

"It's tempting, I'll agree, but it would be wrong. Oh, we could put Tyler away, certainly, but we know that he isn't working alone and I am not at all sure that he would oblige us with names and addresses. He may not even know them. It's a familiar situation; the drug squads face it all the time. They catch a pusher or a courier and there the trail ends. In no time at all the barons have recruited a new pusher and they are that much wiser."

"I can see that, I'm not stupid," de Wet retorted. "What it comes down to is that you can't guarantee that Tyler will talk. If we had him I could give you that assurance."

"I don't doubt it and if Tyler were South African he might well be handed over to you. But he's British. He's our problem and we'll handle it in our own way."

De Wet held back his rejoinder. A slanging match would do no good. He simply had no cards to play. The fact that he had not been transferred probably meant that his own department had nobody to replace him with. He couldn't push his luck by complaining that the British were still being obstinate despite what might have been said and done from above. This was the best he could hope for. "Where is he now?" He sounded as if he expected him to be in the Dorchester.

Without hesitation Randolph said, "I can't tell you that. But it's not very far away and it is a place of our choosing so it was well prepared. Special Branch have a 24-hour watch on every exit and transmissions from each room are being monitored at Scotland Yard. Nothing will be missed, believe me. The only vehicle at the house is also fitted with a transmitter. The house is in a cul-de-sac so nothing on wheels will be passing swiftly by."

"But you can't keep that kind of a stake-out going indefinitely."

"If it collapses then we shall have Tyler and we'll be in the position that you now favour, but as long as we can keep up this charade we stand to gain a great deal more. Tyler has set his sights on half a million pounds and he has no intention of giving away the source of his material — with or without the money. Somehow we have to get around that obstacle and we won't do it by throwing Tyler back in the cells. In the meantime the police will be discreetly checking out every laboratory in the country that has the facilities and expertise to produce this sort of thing — pharmaceutical companies, animal health labs, teaching and research — they'll all be covered."

De Wet was silent for a long time, apparently digesting what Randolph had said. But the words which had silenced him were anonymous; a few hesitant phrases spoken in a voice that was wrought with anxiety . . . *I am making enquiries, Mr Tamala. I am hoping to avoid official channels*. . . . De Wet could hear the recording as if the tape were in his own head. Did it come from a laboratory? Should he now turn it over to this cautious little Englishman? It might be crucial to police enquiries but it might not. Strictly, the recording had been obtained illegally and to avoid embarrassment, if nothing stronger, one did not mention such things when the host country had not been informed. Moreover, the infiltration of the FAM in London was a long-standing and still priceless asset. De Wet found it hard to do or say anything which might, however remotely, put it in jeopardy. He was not a trusting man and his opinion of the British did nothing to change that facet of his nature. Besides, if the voice should call again who knew what it might tell them?

"So you see," Randolph added to bring the man back to attention. "We are not exactly dragging our feet and we are not leaving Tyler in the custody of a single agent. Special Branch have a major role in the operation."

De Wet concluded his deliberations with a sudden sigh. "Very well," he said. "We'll let them get on with it but I hope that from now on we can have daily contact." And that was all he said.

Randolph inclined his head. He had already given that undertaking to his own Director General.

In cases of abduction and kidnapping it is generally believed that time works on the side of the victim. Personal relationships have a chance to develop; time gives humanity a chance. Despite the open-endedness of the assignment Peter Lawson had his orders. When deception was seen to have failed, then and only then, could brutality be tried. But on no account was Tyler to be killed, because others would want to talk to him. For more than a week they had been together, hiding away like convicts on the run. In front of the tiny screen Tyler stooped to fiddle yet again with the controls while Lawson regarded him with deliberate dispassion.

It couldn't be much longer, Lawson told himself, before things came to a head. How would it be, the showdown? He had tried to imagine all the possibilities but knew it was a futile exercise. Once before he had been prepared to torture the truth from a man, but then revenge had been the driving force and violence was the natural expression of his passion. This was different. *Keep feelings out of it*, they had told him. He would try. Only he could do what had to be done and then disappear without raising the cry of police brutality. The police would pick up the pieces and Tyler, if he was capable of speech, might decide to give them a description of the man who called himself Peter; the man he had assumed was working for a communist régime. *And no noisy brawling*, they had cautioned. *Not all your neighbours will be Special Branch.* Lawson fingered the little black cylinder in its holster. There were far more effective products than the Mace but he couldn't appear too sophisticated.

Tyler flipped over the channel in disgust. "Repeat," he said. "There's never anything new." He slumped back on the sofa and glared at Lawson. "How much longer are we going to be cooped up here? They won't learn anything more from that sample, you know. It will be no different from the last one. I'm not staying locked up here for weeks on end while somebody writes a bloody thesis on it. If they want it they know the price. And no way will they pressure me down on that."

Lawson knew he meant it. Tyler had programmed his mind for half a million in a Swiss bank and he probably wasn't capable of accepting anything less. He evidently had that sort of mind.

Swiss banks are equally inflexible when it comes to rules and procedures. Not that Swiss bankers are necessarily saintlier souls of discretion than any other but their ethical code is enforced by law. There were ways around the problem, Lawson had been told, but only as a last resort. In the meantime the word was — stall for time while Special Branch try to track down the source of the sample.

Lawson yawned. "Don't go on at me, I'm not enjoying this either."

"Then tell me who else I can talk to."

"I'll pass any messages, you know that."

"Well you can tell them that whatever game they think they're playing, I'm getting sick of it. Tell them my patience is running out."

"Sure." And when Lawson next went to the telephone he confirmed that the message had got through.

ELEVEN

NERO DID NOT even try to understand. It was not the time for thinking things through. An imminent disaster had miraculously not happened. Perhaps the Russian was a fool. Or maybe his machine wasn't working. Or it could be that he had found the thing and would report it secretly to his own bosses — only an idiot would wait to find out. Anybody with half a brain would get as far away as possible while there was still a chance. Now was the time to run.

It was not much past noon but the streets were a sombre grey beneath heavy rain-cloud. The first few drops had spattered in the dust of the pavement but the deluge was holding back. He hurried along Caledonian Road and turned into Mackenzie Road, glancing back at the corner to see if he was being followed. Around the open door of a pub the smell of beer and hot pies hung thickly in the still, moist air. There was a crush of men at the bar, peering over shoulders, pointing and calling their orders. There came vividly into Nero's mind the image of a street accident he had once seen and he shied away from the kerb, shooting nervous glances at the traffic behind. Nothing was kerb-crawling; nothing looked threatening but fear stirred the imagination. Fear was a demon which drove the body and deranged the mind. Why was he almost running, breathless in the midday streets? Why had he left the bus route without a thought, blindly obeying the urge to escape? Deliberately he slowed his pace and began to control his breathing. The muscles of his legs were hurting, there were spasms every time his feet slapped down from his built-up heels. He looked back again at the traffic, this time hoping to see a taxi. The rain began falling in big, heavy drips, hesitantly at first and then with abandon. People scurried for cover, standing under awnings and in shop doorways, knowing that the downpour wouldn't last. Nero dallied for a few seconds, his back to a wall. Water poured in front of him like a huge tattered screen hung from a stone coping above. A youth strolled past, his head held high and a fixed smile upon his face. Long brown hair streamed over his shoulders and clung like seaweed to his sodden jacket. Nero moved on, trying to keep clear of the hissing, spraying traffic.

He had gone less than a hundred metres when a passing van suddenly slowed and drew alongside. Nero's eyes widened and he veered across the pavement. It was an ageing Volkswagen richly blotched with red metal primer. The nearside window went down and a grinning face appeared.

"Hey Nero! You look like a drowned rat, man."

Nero stopped in his tracks. His pastel blue suit was dark with water. His soaking trousers, once neatly pressed and flared, were wrapped round his legs like so much lagging. He blinked for a moment and then said, "Charlie!" And he began to laugh.

"Well c'mon, get in the back, don't stand around."

Nero rolled back the side door and climbed in gratefully, still giggling. The driver shook his head and slipped back into the traffic stream. Charlie twisted round in his seat.

"Where the hell you going to, Nero?"

He thought quickly. "If you can drop me home that would be good."

"You're not working?"

"Sure I am. I left some papers at my place, that's all. We need them at the office."

Charlie nodded. "No problem." He turned to the driver. "You can go by Nero's place, Jim?"

"If this thing can float." He was hunched over the wheel, peering at the road through a streaky patch which was the only place where the wiper made contact with the glass. "You got a smoke on you?"

Nero held out a slim cigarette case. "Still dry too."

They all took one and handed round Nero's gold lighter. "What are you doing these days. Charlie?"

The driver sniggered. "Don't ask him," he warned.

Charlie grinned, proud and sheepish at the same time. "Oh, I make out, doing this and that."

More sniggering. "This and that!"

143

Charlie poked him with a rigid finger "You keep your tiny mind on the steering, boatman."

Nero laughed loudly, thankful for the banter. This was reality, a repellent for secret fears. It was the safe and familiar bed that you found when waking chased away the troubling dreams. "Okay, I won't ask," he chortled.

They made their way eastwards. Nero's apartment was a ground floor unit in a row bordered to the point of being barricaded by unroadworthy vehicles.

"You fellas coming in?"

They were both emphatic. "Not now, Nero. We have things to do. See you around, okay?"

"Okay, thanks for the ride. See you, Charlie."

The VW pulled away with a noise like an amplified old sewing machine and Nero made little giant's strides across the streaming gutter. The rain had eased to a patter and the leaden sky had relented enough to let through a silvery glow. He let himself in and closed the door quietly, almost furtively, as guilt and fear crept from the silence to play again at the controls of his mind. Worry was reality once more and the interlude with Charlie became the dream.

Nero had never been happy about hiding the money. Hidden cash was always a worry but what else to do? Banking meant records, explanations to the tax authorities, solid evidence for anyone who might get his or her hands on the printouts. Illicit money in a local bank account seemed no less worrying than stored cash but there wasn't enough to be worth smuggling abroad. It wasn't all *that* much, not quite six thousand pounds in fact, so it had stayed hidden while it steadily accumulated and he remained undecided.

First he went to the wardrobe and pulled a small suitcase from the bottom. He flung it open on the bed and hurriedly folded in three or four shirts without taking them off their wire hangers. A lightweight suit and extra trousers went on top, then a white roll-neck sweater, socks and pants. Papers came next. He had them to hand in a drawer of a dressing-table: passport, a bank book, two insurance policies, some receipts and letters. He stuffed them in the case and took stock of his belongings around the room as he kicked away his shoes and peeled off his wet clothes. In a matter of seconds he had changed into a fawn casual outfit with a pink shirt and two-tone shoes. He was still damp because he had not towelled down, but the dry clothes felt good. He snatched up a small leather cufflinks box, flipped the lid to check that his gold bracelets and links were inside, then darted into the bathroom for his electric shaver. He hesitated over a cassette recorder and finally left it in favour of a small transistor radio which fitted more readily in the suitcase.

The money was hidden in a cavity of an old fireplace — long since disused and fitted with an electric heater. He dropped to his knees as if in supplication to the imitation coals and reached through a gap to the brickwork behind. A loose brick had to be edged out at one end until there was enough purchase for a straight pull. It was awkward, but less of a bother than lifting out the heater because that was bolted to a backboard which blocked most of the old grate. The brick came free and his fingers closed on the tin cans which protected his little hoard. They were coffee tins and he levered off the lids with his door key for a sight of the money. It was all there, in tightly-rolled wads of ten pound notes. He began to pull them out, intending to carry the money in his pockets, but then he changed his mind and pushed only five notes into his wallet. The rest he returned to the cans and stuffed them into the loaded suitcase, levelling the heap before forcing down the lid. Nero then took a last look round and made for the door. There was a raincoat on a hook there which he thought to collect on his way out.

He never did collect the coat because standing beside it, silent and motionless, was a tall man with a lopsided smile.

Nero stopped, aghast, in mid stride then spun on his heel and ran to the back door. The waiting figure calmly unfolded its arms. The back door was also covered. The man was more Nero's size but he held a pistol. Nero clutched his case to his chest as if it could shield him as he backed away. Not a word had been spoken until Nero began to bluster.

"Who the hell are you? What do you want? You have no right to be in here."

But he might have been a deaf mute for all the notice they took as they closed in on him.

★

Christian Collins stirred in his bed or, more accurately, her bed, at 6 a.m. the following morning — just a few minutes before the alarm was supposed to wake him. He stopped the buzzer before it went off and twisted round to look at Sue who was sound asleep and appeared to be in exactly the same position as when he had climbed off her seven hours before. It had not been all that wonderful last night, though neither of them would know why. Who could understand such things? Hormones, blood sugar levels, biorhythms, booze — this loving business was all too bloody subtle and complicated. He studied her for a moment as she lay there. She was breathing in through her nose and out through her mouth so that she puffed rather than snored, her lips parting slightly with every outbreath. He smiled and slipped out of bed to start the day. When he came back he was half dressed and carried tea things on a tray. He finished dressing and woke her just before he had to leave.

She sat up and mechanically took the teacup in both hands. "What time is it?"

"Time I was gone. I'm on earlies if you recall.'

"Earlies?"

"My shift."

"Oh, that. Glorified eavesdropping if you ask me."

"Well luckily nobody is asking you and if ever they do I hope you will remember not to know anything."

"I don't consider that I do know anything."

"You know more than you should and that's for sure." He kissed her on the forehead, slopping tea into the saucer. "See you later."

"Have fun."

He *had* told her too much, but no real details. He couldn't see the harm in it and one had to say something if only to explain why one couldn't say more. It was either that or make up a pack of lies.

It had been a quiet night in the records room, he learned when he got there. That was not surprising because they had never picked up a call from Tamala's office line during the night. The silence of the previous day had been unusual but not deeply disturbing because there had been a couple of calls earlier in the day to indicate that Tamala would be out for at least part of the afternoon and it wasn't hard to believe that there had been no incoming calls. It was therefore nearly 30 hours after Vlasov's sweep that Collins felt it necessary to report the silence.

De Wet took the news with nothing more than a tightening of the lips. "Nothing? No clicks? Nothing at all?"

"Nothing."

"Go back and listen now. I'll try it."

Collins went back to records and fitted the headphones again while he waited for de Wet to dial the number. Before dialling, de Wet opened the top drawer of his desk and pulled out a thick rubber disc on a long flex. He pressed the rubber over the mouthpiece of the phone. It fitted snugly. The flex led to a pocket-sized micro-processor which remained in the drawer. He moved a tiny selector switch and dialled the FAM number. In Tamala's office the girl answered. "Hello."

"I'd like to speak to Mr Tamala, please." There was no disguising the South African accent but at the other end of the line de Wet's voice was distinctly feminine. Nor did it sound more mechanical than any other voice on the line; the device altered sound frequencies without changing other qualities of speech.

"Mr Tamala is not available just now."

"Well, is Mr Boko there, please?"

"No, I am sorry, he is not here."

"Do you know when he will be back?"

"I don't know. Can I take a message?"

"It doesn't matter, I'll call again."

De Wet uncoupled the convertor and abstractedly read the 'made in Israel' lettering while he stroked his moustache with the tips of his well-kept fingers. The bug had been discovered. He felt depressingly certain of it.

In records Collins was still in headphones when de Wet appeared and the blank look on his face confirmed the worst. "Did you get through?" He lifted one earpiece as he spoke.

De Wet nodded. "A girl answered."

"Oh well, that's it then. I got none of it."

It was another hour before de Wet could contact Danny Meester to pass the news. Each knew the other's thoughts and de Wet was prepared for Meester's outburst. It did not come. Meester simply said "I see". But the effort nearly choked him.

In an unmarked police car near the city of Cambridge two CID men were feeling less than confident about their assignment.

"A bit bloody vague," said Armstrong.

"Typical," Lund affirmed. "Do you reckon the Super knew any more?"

"I doubt it. It's another of these intelligence jobs. They wouldn't tell the coppers anything at all if they didn't have to. It's the 'need to know' principle gone mad."

"But who puts the classification on these things? It has to be a joint decision doesn't it? Our blokes and security."

"Unless the politicians get in on the act."

"Can't see the politics in this one."

"We are not intended to, are we. It must rate pretty big, though, it's a nationwide op."

"You weren't here when that chap Chandler disappeared, were you?"

"No, but I've read the report."

"That's all I've done. I wasn't on it myself. It's over a year now."

"Might be a connection somewhere."

Lund shrugged. "Nothing obvious. He had a row with his girlfriend on Friday night and vanished on the Saturday. Just happened to work at Nettiscombe."

"In the research division."

"Oh, it's possible. Anything's possible but you heard what the Super said — name Tyler not to be disclosed and no known connection with any British pharmaceutical firm."

"Well, we'll give 'em the easy questions routine and leave it at that if nothing comes out of it. It's all that's expected of us."

Lund sighed and turned to watch the scenic offerings that were coming into view. "I suppose the sensible thing is to be philosophical. We've got a ride in the country, a simple job to do, it's a nice day, the hawthorn's in flower, what have we got to complain about?"

Armstrong grinned at him. "I've tried all that. It lasts about ten minutes generally."

With Armstrong gunning the Rover rather faster than Lund was trying to be in the mood for, they reached the laboratories in less than half an hour. Together they walked from the parking area across the immaculate frontage of lawn and shrubbery to the white stone steps which led to the front office and enquiries desk.

"Ever been here at all, Bill?"

Armstrong shook his head. "Considering the size of the place they manage to keep a very low profile."

"No contacts then."

A girl came down the steps and hurried past them, fishing in her bag to make sure she had her car key. In step they marched on but with the timing of a military eyes-right they took in every detail of her firm young figure. "No," Armstrong muttered wistfully. "No contact."

"Armstrong," he announced to the woman on the visitors desk. "And Lund. We have an appointment with Mr Forbes-Milne."

She looked at them as if they were not what she expected and she kept staring at them as she pressed a button and moved her lips behind the handset of an intercom. And then she said "this way please", just as she had been told to do.

Forbes-Milne greeted them cautiously but made them comfortable in the club chairs of his office suite. The policemen glanced at each other in a silent comment on the contrast with their own cramped and shoddy little work-space back at HQ.

"Now, what's all this about?"

Armstrong resisted the temptation to say he only wished he knew and said instead, "We are not in a position to say very much at present, I'm afraid. We're at a very preliminary stage of the enquiry and it's really just a case of eliminating some of the possibilities . . . sharpening the focus so to speak. Basically, we have reason to believe that a dangerous virus culture has fallen into the wrong hands and we're very anxious to find out where it came from."

Forbes-Milne, nearly sixty and very sure of himself began to shake his head but Armstrong continued, giving him no chance to say 'not from here'.

"Of course, we don't expect you to know anything about it but I would be glad if we could just look at the problem together; you might be able to advise us."

"But have you reason to suppose that Nettiscombe is involved in any way?"

"None whatever, sir. But we can't cross it off the list in advance. We must at least consider it together. I doubt if, in this country, there is any such thing as a disreputable pharmaceutical company, but the stuff's come from somewhere and we just have to follow a process of elimination. In your case it shouldn't be much more than a formality. I'm sure you have very strict safety precautions."

"Indeed we do, Inspector. But, you know, the blood of an infected animal or person could be collected by any lunatic who wanted to spread disease. It wouldn't have to come from a laboratory at all."

Armstrong scratched his neck and glanced at Lund whose face was a blank. "We are policemen, not scientists," he said unnecessarily. "But it's our understanding that this particular virus must have come from a laboratory because of the way it has been cultured. According to the forensic boffins it had been specially . . . refined in some way."

Forbes-Milne frowned. "And has it been identified?"

"We've been informed that it's similar to the rabies virus."

The first faint trace of concern passed over the carefully composed features. "Well, we do manufacture a rabies vaccine as you no doubt know, but we enforce the most stringent standards of safety. Good heavens, we can trace every individual phial of every batch from production to delivery. Batch numbers are recorded by the dispensing chemists so even the end users can be located."

The Inspector was nodding understandingly even as the other spoke but then he said, "I don't doubt it, sir, but what's to stop somebody from collecting a bit of extra serum and processing it separately in some way? It wouldn't be recorded as part of any batch so it would be outside your routine screening procedures wouldn't it?"

Forbes-Milne hesitated for a moment. "Inspector, we don't leave infective materials lying about like bricks on a building site. You are welcome to visit our laboratories and even to go into the restricted and quarantine areas but you will be required to wear special clothing and you will be accompanied every step of the way by a supervisor. Ask all the questions you can think of and if you can see any slackness in our security I shall be glad to hear of it. But you might also talk to the ministry inspectors because they come down here often enough to do exactly the same thing."

"You know, that's a very good point," Armstrong said approvingly. "If the ministry chaps, who know what they are looking at, are satisfied with the system, who am I to find fault?"

Forbes-Milne spread his hands without comment.

"And yet, as I was briefed," Armstrong went on, "in police custody there is a virus culture which our own consultant scientists have told us is extremely dangerous and was a threat to public safety. I can tell you that it was taken from somebody who should have had no access to material of that sort and no knowledge of such things. So where did it come from? How did he get it? Let's suppose that the ministry inspectors assure us that every laboratory in the country has a first class record on security. Where do we go from there?"

"Well, where does he *say* it came from?"

Armstrong suddenly grinned. "It's not my case, sir, but I think you can assume that whatever's been said can't be taken too seriously. The obvious concern, of course, is that there is more of the stuff about and others might be involved with it."

Forbes-Milne drew a deep breath and looked at his watch again. "I really can't help you, inspector. I don't know what to suggest. I'm sorry."

Ignoring an enquiring glance from Lund, Armstrong made no move to leave. "I'm sorry to have to bother you with it," he said with some sincerity. "But I'm afraid a lot of people are going to have to be troubled before we run this thing down. Now, let's start thinking about individuals. It might be worth checking the records with personnel and talking to the heads of departments. Has anybody recently been dismissed? Anybody have reason to bear a grudge? Any odd behaviour been reported? Any newcomers who are still on probation, as it were? You had a chap disappear about a year ago, still on the missing list. Who replaced him? Might be worth having a word there, for instance."

Forbes-Milne slowly shook his head as he called up personnel and arranged for Messrs Armstrong and Lund to be introduced to the heads of departments.

★

By about the time that the two Cambridge CID men were ready to leave Nettiscombe, one Raymond (Birdie) Birdwood was concluding a solitary fight against indecision on the streets of London E1. Birdie hated indecision; it made him feel smaller than he really was. Not that he suffered from any delusions of grandeur at the best of times, but at least he liked to be able to hold up his head among his peers and say that he remained free and solvent because he had a good eye for a chance and the confidence to take it when it came up. Birdie prided himself on being an opportunist and he felt annoyed to find himself dithering, like a kid on his first job.

Still, better cautious than reckless, he reasoned. The Old Bill were up to all sorts of tricks these days. Saying they were more concerned about preventing crime than catching criminals was a load of eyewash. Without crime they'd all be out of a job and they weren't above dangling the bait where temptation showed results. But this wasn't a bait, Birdie decided. Nobody was watching it. He crossed the street and walked purposefully towards the Vauxhall. Having made up his mind he was now totally committed to the part of a rightful owner returning to his parked car. It was disastrous to look furtive. People noticed things like that and remembered your face.

Birdie's face was not the sort that made much impression in the ordinary run of things. He had a pasty complexion and a discreet moustache, medium brown eyes and thinning brown hair. Nor was there anything remarkable about the rest of him. He was rather less than average height, somewhat lighter than medium build and not quite shabbily dressed. Birdie Birdwood was a nondescript. He knew it and made the most of it.

He allowed himself one swift glance up and down the street, a perfectly natural traffic check, before slipping into the driver's seat. The ignition key was already in place. An ornate Turk's head knot in red leather hung from the key ring. It was that which had first caught his attention. Birdie pulled away smoothly, relieved to see the fuel indicator climb steadily to the half-full mark. Phase one was under way. If he were picked up now he'd be convicted of stealing a car but it would be a minor crime committed on impulse. When the petrol ran out he would have abandoned it, he could say. Kids were doing it all the time.

There had been a period when he had kept stolen cars in his

home garage overnight and then in his lock-up under the railway arches not far from the Royal Mint, but he preferred not to think about that now. He wouldn't dream of taking such stupid risks these days. This time he drove directly to Thommo's Tune-up & Wheel Balance which was a father and son establishment specializing in small jobs which could be done quickly. It took him about fifteen minutes to get there and he drove straight round to the back. All he needed was a place where different cars were to be seen going in and out all the time. All he wanted from Thommo and his son was a blind eye. Five minutes later he drove out again with different number plates. Phase two.

Phase two had to be taken more seriously. If he were to be picked up now it would be hard to deny that he was involved in planned car theft. But the chances of being caught in phase two were remote as long as he kept to popular car models in standard colours. With different number plates there was then nothing to distinguish a missing car from thousands of others on the roads.

Birdie drove carefully eastwards along Commercial Road and then turned north into the streets of Stepney. He stopped at a phone box and made a local call. It was little more than a formality but it was one of Joe Stoddart's rules that all deliveries should first be cleared by phone. It was another of Joe's rules that the plates must first be changed so that no vehicle was ever delivered with the original registration number.

"Joe? It's Birdie. Listen, I've got a very nice Cavalier to show you. She's a beauty. Okay just now is it? Right then, I'm on my way."

It was worth going along with Joe's way of doing things. He was one of the straightest crooks in the business. Always cash on the nail and no nonsense. But he wasn't a man to cross. Birdie took a good look up and down the street before leaving the booth. It was force of habit.

Stoddart was on the phone when Birdie arrived and he waved a hand from the window of his cubby-hole office. Birdie nosed the car into the space indicated, climbed out and patted the bonnet ostentatiously. Within the week, he knew, it would be back on the road with yet another change of plates, a new colour-scheme and very convincing documents.

Stoddart was a short, thickset man with a black beard. He nodded amiably enough at Birdie but didn't look overjoyed to see him. Together they stood and looked appraisingly at the car.

"Where did you find it?"

"Wappin'"

"Know anything about it?"

"No. Been there a few hours. Key in."

Stoddart glanced at him briefly as he prowled around the vehicle to see if there were conspicuous dents or scratches. Somebody in the workshop was whistling out of tune: piercing notes above the background din. Then it was drowned by the screech of an angle grinder. Stoddart leant into the car to read the mileage, removing the ignition key as he did so. He examined the red leather knot curiously then pulled it off with a deft twist and handed it to Birdie who pocketed it without comment.

"Have you checked the boot?"

Birdie shook his head. "Haven't had a chance."

The screeching stopped for a few moments and the workshop suddenly seemed very quiet. Stoddart went to the rear and unlocked the boot. He lifted it just as the grinding restarted. If he said anything at all Birdie did not catch the words, but he saw Stoddart's lips move as his face was suddenly contorted with shock. In the boot even the position of Nero's body was strangely unnatural. The knees were drawn up tightly but one arm was stiffly stretched down the length of the back, palm upwards. A green plastic bag was wrapped about the head but, from the collapsed and crumpled outline and the sticky mess which surrounded it, it was obvious that there was no head.

Stoddart slammed the boot shut and rubbed his hands on his overalls as if he had touched the thing.

"Get it out of here! Get it OUT."

Birdie just stood there, his eyes wide and his lips trembling as he tried to find words. Stoddart shoved the key into his hand and bundled him into the driver's seat.

"Just get out," he yelled. "Drive. Drive." He said it again and again until Birdie went through the motions and the car pulled away with a gnashing of badly changed gears.

TWELVE

It pleased the newsmen that the body could not, at first, be identified. A mystery in the news is always to the good although, as is so often the case, it was largely a forgotten mystery by the time the police came up with a name. For Danny Meester there never was a mystery. He had no doubt, when he read the lurid little caption, that the name of Nero would be announced sooner or later. "It's him for sure," he told de Wet with some bitterness. "It leaves us with nothing."

Frits de Wet had to agree. "What the hell are they playing at," he said with quiet ferocity. "The Special Branch, the fools at the Foreign Office, all of them. They have had our man for days. This thing should be finished and done with."

"Well, it's up to them completely now. We have no handle on it at all." Meester spoke with a trace of sarcastic satisfaction.

De Wet glared at his watch. "I shall be seeing our little English gentleman in about an hour." He made it sound like a threat.

The English gentleman was at that moment going through a list of reports which had been collated and supplied by Commander Daintry. There were seven of them and they represented a short list of 'possibles' from the two dozen laboratories which had been treated to a cursory once-over by Special Branch detectives. A firm in Surrey headed the list because of generally lax security and an unusual and passionately-held philosophy on the part of the senior research biochemist. Carried to its logical conclusions his credo would have led to the experimental animal pens being filled entirely with *Homo sapiens*. Nettiscombe Laboratories was third from the bottom and was included only because a sectional head of research had seemed unduly disturbed by the line of questioning. That head of research was Dr Jonathon Jolliffe.

"I'd say all these are worth a closer look wouldn't you, Bill?" Randolph said without looking up.

Fletcher agreed but with no great conviction.

"You don't sound very sure." Randolph was now giving his full attention.

"Oh, it's not that I disagree but I wonder if we are going to have time to do much more. I don't think Tyler is going to wait much longer. If he doesn't get his money he'll do something, James. Things will be brought to a head."

"Well, we are not exactly wasting time, Bill. You can tell Daintry that I agree with his assessment. Ask him to go ahead with the deeper probes exactly as he suggests. You may also tell him that if nothing comes of it we'll call off the charade and he can pull Tyler in again. Even de Wet might be happy with that news."

But Frits de Wet was rarely seen to be happy at work. Expressions of joy did not fit easily into his professional image. Besides, he didn't feel very carefree when he met Randolph that morning at the Foreign Office.

"How long will all this take?" he asked testily.

"A day or two, I should think. And then, with or without his associates, we'll have Tyler back in the cells."

For several long seconds de Wet said nothing. He stroked a finger-tip along his moustache and then removed his spectacles. He angled them in the light as if he were looking for the slightest smear on the shining lenses. "It is just possible," he said eventually, "that we have a voice from one of those laboratories." He looked squarely at Randolph then, and produced a tape cassette from his pocket. "Is there somewhere we can listen to this?"

Randolph began to collect the papers that they had been looking at together. "It's a standard cassette, is it?"

"Yes. The original is on a spool."

"Then I'll have a little portable sent down."

He went to the door and spoke to the man who was standing outside. A few minutes later a cassette recorder was brought in. It was a Japanese, mass-produced model with a sticker which said ROOM 13 DO NOT REMOVE. The messenger returned to his post outside and Randolph plugged in the unit. "Seems to work. Try it."

Randolph stood back while de Wet slipped in the cassette. Together they stood staring at the machine as they waited for the sound. Conway's voice was slightly distorted but the words were perfectly clear. De Wet glanced sideways at the Englishman but Randolph remained staring at the moving tape in the tiny plastic window. The voice stopped.

"Any more?" he said softly.

"No, that's all."

Randolph prodded the rewind button and listened again. Finally he switched off and looked hard at the South African. The questions were there to be read.

"We picked it up a few days ago," de Wet said unflinchingly. "We had a little helper in the FAM office."

"But this was recorded off the line."

"That's right. Our man put the bug in."

"And now?"

"Not any more. They found it."

"What about your *little helper*?"

De Wet was removing his cassette. "No word." He dropped the cassette in its case and waggled it between finger and thumb. "The question now is whether this call came from one of your laboratory boys."

"The question is why you didn't let Daintry have that before he had the labs checked out!" Randolph said icily. "You might have saved a lot of time."

But de Wet was not easily discomposed. "We might have saved a lot more time if they hadn't found the bug. They'll be very careful for a while now. The Ivans will make sure of that."

Randolph turned away. What was done was done; he was not a man to show temper. "Daintry will need the best recording possible. He should have the original."

"There's nothing wrong with this one if you play it on a decent machine. But no problem, he can have the original, I'll deliver it to him myself. In return I expect to be allowed to talk to Tyler."

For a moment there may have been exasperation in Randolph's eyes but he merely blinked once or twice and said: "Talk to Tyler when? Where?"

"As soon as you pull him in again. I have my own questions to ask."

"Oh, I see." Randolph showed little of the relief he felt either. "Be in on the interrogation, you mean. As long as Daintry has no objection I don't see why not. All the cards should be on the table by then."

"Christ, I should hope so."

"He will need that recording right away. The follow-up on the labs is already being organized."

"He will have it in about half an hour."

"It might also save time if you would let me take this one. We have our own expertise on voice analysis."

The Afrikaner hesitated for a moment then shrugged and handed him the cassette. "I'll be in touch tomorrow, then. Unless I hear from you first."

Randolph asked the messenger to see him out, and when they had gone he put the tape back in the player, sat down and listened again, very carefully and thoughtfully. He played it through twice then pocketed the cassette and went upstairs to use the telephone in Clive Forrest's office. For ten minutes he spoke earnestly to Commander Daintry at New Scotland Yard, then he left the building and returned directly to his own headquarters at Eland House.

"Something has come up, Bill," he announced as soon as he got there. "We've had a little windfall."

"You've also had five calls and three telexes which need attention," Fletcher said, pointing to his desk. "And Sadie wanted to talk to you as well."

"I know, I saw her on the way in." Randolph picked up the papers on his blotter, read them quickly and put them down again. "They'll keep for an hour or two. Listen Bill, I've just left de Wet and got something that we have to move on. Now tell me, are you still in touch with Monty Tucker?"

Monty Tucker was a misfit; a man without a niche. It was hard to say whether he was not suited for anything or whether he was reasonably competent in so many roles that dabbling was his true path through life. He had been, among other things, a soldier, a publican, a fishing tour operator, a schoolmaster and twice married. He liked his booze but was not an alcoholic or even a drunk. He was not politically active but firmly believed that British was best — or when it wasn't it was because British people were not really trying.

As a raconteur he was excellent, although it was harder to get him started now than it had been in his younger days. He did not see himself as an entertainer and the theatre was one way of life which he had never tried. "Miserable buggers, comedians," he had once observed. "Unnatural, you see. Fun has to be a spontaneous thing otherwise it's a strain." Yet times without number an appreciative, and not always inebriated, company had told him that he ought to be on the stage, for Monty Tucker could not only tell a good tale when he wanted to, he was also a very accomplished mimic.

It was early lunchtime when he got to the pub and by the time Fletcher arrived he was already standing squarely at the bar holding a pint. Fletcher watched him from the door while he took off his coat and hung it up. Tucker hadn't changed in the last two years. He was still a slightly overweight figure and still wore a check suit and suede shoes. He turned as Fletcher approached and showed that he also still wore a full face of hair. Bright eyes twinkled with recognition from deep sockets beneath black, bushy brows. A full beard and moustache presented broad grey stripes in the dark frame of hair which curled about his ears and all but covered the rest of his face. Fletcher beamed his greeting and instantly saw what had once prompted the remark that Tucker resembled nothing so much as a skunk peering out of a bear's arse.

"Monty, you old devil. Good to see you; what there is to be seen, that is."

Tucker's whiskers broadened. "Daren't shave now, Bill. Dread to think what it looks like underneath. What are you having?"

"What you've got looks good to me."

Tucker ordered another pint of bitter and together they moved away from the bar.

"We'll have to drop these pretty damn quick, Monty. We can't talk here."

Tucker, with his top lip in his mug, wiggled his eyebrows in reply. A few minutes later both men were on their way to King Charles Street, SW1.

If Clive Forest was surprised or even curious about Monty Tucker he gave no sign of it. He had been told what to expect and Bill Fletcher was well known to him. The basement room was empty, secure and already equipped with portable (but this time hi-fi) recording paraphernalia.

Fletcher looked it over. "Do you know much about this sort of gadgetry?"

Tucker didn't.

"Neither do I but this thing seems basic enough." He took the cassette from his breast pocket and slotted it into a separate player. "Now, listen to this, Monty. Listen carefully now."

Tucker listened intently to the brief conversation and when he heard the final click of a telephone he made his pronouncement. "One's English, probably from a minor public school, and the foreigner sounds like a gentleman of non-reflective countenance."

Fletcher smiled. "We know who they are, Monty. The thing is, can you do the voices?"

"I should think so; with a bit of practice. What do you want me to say?"

Fletcher unfolded a sheet of paper. "Not very much. Just a few words in fact. Try this."

"I'll need to practise a bit. Let me say the same words a time or two before I try different ones."

He ran the tape back and played it through again while he listened with his eyes closed. When it ended he looked at Fletcher in an odd sort of way and said, "Look, do you mind buggering off somewhere. It's this spontaneity thing. I'm not good at doing things to order and you standing there makes it worse somehow."

For an astonished moment Fletcher just stared but then he collected his wits and said, "Of course, stupid of me. Putting you off, of course. I'll go where I can smoke a pipe. There's a chap outside, so just let him know when you want me back. The door's soundproof, by the way." And on the outside Fletcher spoke a few words to the man before moving on up the corridor. He shook his head slightly as he went and breathed a few syllables to himself as well. "Unbelievable," he heard himself say. "Monty Tucker, shy."

It was nearly an hour before Fletcher was called back, by which time Tucker was full of confidence again.

"Had to do a lot of rubbing out but I think it's all right now." He started the machine and they heard it through. It lasted for only seventeen seconds and at the end of it Fletcher clapped his thick hands in appreciation.

"Bloody marvellous, Monty. Perfect."

Tucker flashed his teeth. "Tricky thing, imitating a recording. The tape makes a difference. You have to allow for it."

"You've done wonders." Fletcher was quickly packing away the tapes. "Er, I can't make this very official," he said. "But we do have a little consultancy fund and I'll try to make sure they aren't too stingy with it."

"Ah, well, that would be appreciated." He looked at his watch. "I wonder if you have time for the other half, Bill. They're still open."

Fletcher wobbled his cheeks. "I wish I had but I've got people waiting for this. There will be another time, I don't doubt."

"Good," Tucker said. "I hope so."

At New Scotland Yard Commander Daintry, acting on Randolph's call, had prepared well for de Wet's arrival. By the time the South African brought in the original tape the technicians were ready to duplicate it and an officer had been detailed to organize deliveries by the fastest possible means. Use of the radio for tape transmission had been reluctantly ruled out after consultation with the technicians. Two copies went on the London-to-Glasgow express, three went by air and two, including the one to Cambridge, were delivered by road. The Cambridge copy was passed immediately to Armstrong and Lund.

"Well at least we've got a clear directive this time," Lund remarked. "I mean we know what we're looking for."

"They still haven't given much away though, have they. Put a face to the voice and bring him in for questioning. If he won't come get his details to the Super and you'll have a warrant within the hour. Wonderful. We still don't even know what he should be charged with."

Lund sniffed. "I expect we'll find out if he turns up on our patch."

Dr Jonathon Jolliffe was, as usual, sitting at his expansive desk with his forehead resting on his fingertips. From time to time he would put a white lab coat over his grey suit and stalk out into the laboratories to discuss some point or other with one of his research staff. But, as a rule, Jolliffe preferred communication by the written word or, better still, by numbers. Conversation did not come easily to him and he did not trust it in others. People said things they did not really mean and would not be prepared to write down. And then they forgot they'd said them. Tape recorders ought to have appealed to him but he regarded them with suspicion — perhaps because he was just not comfortable with them. He frowned severely when personnel asked him to go up to the main block interview room because the police were back. His lips parted in a click of irritation when he heard that they wanted him to listen to a tape recording. But as the request came through the office of the executive director, Forbes-Milne, he knew it would only cause more trouble if he said he was too busy. Even so, he would tell them how busy he was. They should know that.

Probably Jolliffe himself did not realize what really bothered him as he made his way to the main block. True, he was very busy but he was always engrossed in his work and was not normally so put out by interruptions. Confounded policemen again, he fumed. All week there had been one distraction after another. But beneath his private bluster, perhaps beyond the reach of his own thoughts, the director of research was troubled by a lack of confidence.

Jolliffe was a good scientist; not brilliant but more than competent. He led his research team successfully, too. Led them but never really got to know them for, at the common level of personal relationships, Jolliffe began to feel uneasy. He tended to stop short of the ordinary social intercourse that lay just outside the line of duty. It made no difference, he believed, to the running of the department. An efficient working relationship could be based purely on the requirements of the job.

All the same, there were occasions when Jolliffe found himself wondering what sort of life some of his scientists went home to. Not just the younger ones either: old Maurice Slattery was an extraordinary fellow. What on earth was he like with his family? But the young ones were the most difficult to understand. Look at Vernon! And Miss Bannister; not at all the sort of girl one would expect to hold a first in organic chemistry. And then there was Conway — whatever was the matter with him?

If there was going to be a scientific scandal bad enough to interest the police he fervently hoped that it would not turn out to be somebody from his section. But very deep down he feared that it could be.

Detective Inspector Armstrong was unimpressed by people who looked at their watches and said how busy they were. Jolliffe was the fourth that day and he had been to the staff canteen for lunch —which was more than coppers could manage.

"Shan't keep you many minutes, sir," he said with a heavy glance at Lund. "But we have to ask if you've had any further thoughts about the matter we discussed last time."

Jolliffe gave a single sideways turn of his shiny head. "No, I'm afraid I still can't help you there." It was very final and just what both policemen expected. Forbes-Milne had said exactly the same thing.

Armstrong nodded as if that were one formality disposed of, then he turned to Lund who had the recorder.

"We have a short recording here, sir," Lund said on cue. "I'd like you to listen very carefully and tell us if you recognize the voice."

And this time, before the sound-track was half-way through, Armstrong and Lund knew they had struck a nerve.

Jolliffe stiffened and lifted his hand in a sudden gesture before he began to stroke the fringe of hair at the back of his neck. When the voice stopped he asked, "Is there any more?"

"No, that's all."

"May I hear it again?"

Lund did the replay.

"I can't be sure, you know," he said as soon as the replay finished, "but I think that's Ralph Conway's voice." And he looked as if he had just made a confession.

"Conway?" Armstrong and Lund were suddenly very attentive.

"He works in my research unit."

"Is he there now?"

"Yes. He's been taking sick leave lately but he's with us today."

"What, er, what sort of chap is he? Will he be co-operative with us do you think?"

Jolliffe appeared to contemplate for a moment then he got to his feet and said, "Well he certainly won't be violent if that's what you are thinking. He's rather a quiet, reserved young man. Would you like me to send him along?"

"No," Armstrong said quickly. "No, don't do that, doctor. Thank you. I think the best thing is for us to come with you to your unit and then you can just point him out to us."

And it occurred to Jolliffe that they were afraid Conway might run away. He found even the thought distasteful — as if his unit were now to be involved in some street game of cops and robbers. But, clinging the more firmly to his own dignity, he did as the policeman asked.

From his bench Conway saw them appear in Jolliffe's office. At first he felt no more than what had become a familiar tension at the sight of strangers on the threshold of his territory. They were standing and were in clear view above the half-panelled wall of the office. There were reflections on the windows but he could see them looking in his direction. Jolliffe was talking. The other two were staring. Conway dragged his eyes back to the blur of figures on his pad and when next he looked up one of the strangers was leaving. The tension ebbed a little. But then it came back with a surge. Jolliffe was coming into the lab and the other man was staring through the glass.

It was the grey suit that signalled danger; Jolliffe rarely came into the laboratory without his white coat. When he turned between the benches into Conway's aisle the scientist knew that he was about to be summoned. He knew that Jolliffe was coming to fetch him, to take him to the stranger. It had to be the police.

"Ah, Ralph, er, someone to see you."

"Police," Conway said woodenly, and the sound seemed to stay in his throat.

"Ah, yes, actually." Jolliffe glanced around to see who was taking notice, but Conway had his eyes fixed on the man behind the glass. It did not occur to him to try to escape. He did not consider that the other man might be waiting outside the back door or that the third door might be locked. He just started walking towards the office. He was aware that the others were staring, curiously, but he didn't turn aside or respond in any way because they were of no

164

account, of no more importance than flies on the wall. Nothing was important any more.

There was no emotion on Armstrong's face, only interest. "I'm Detective Inspector Armstrong, Dr Conway," he said. "We're making some enquiries that I've reason to think you can help us with. So I'd like you to come into town with us and answer a few questions at the police station."

"Now?"

"That's right. I know Dr Jolliffe can spare you for a while."

So it was happening. It was all happening and Conway began to feel strangely like an observer.

"What is it about?" he heard himself say. He had to know, he had to be certain. He tried to clear his throat. "Questions about what?"

"We can discuss all that at the station," Armstrong said smoothly.

"Can't you tell me anything now?"

"Not really, no. They have all the details down there. And you don't have to say anything either but I should warn you that anything you do say . . ."

"Do I have to come, then?"

Armstrong's features hardened. "We could make it that way, yes."

Conway flapped a hand lamely. "I'll clear my bench."

"No need for that I'm sure," Armstrong said with a loaded glance at Jolliffe.

"No, no, of course. We'll take care of your things."

And so Conway was led meekly to the police car where Lund joined him in the back seat.

He was surprised at how calm he felt. He was aware only of a curious detachment. It was as if he were already beyond the reach of any further events. He noticed the inquisitive face of the gate man as they drove out of the compound and he actually felt like laughing at him. The sense of release was euphoric. He felt free, not captive.

"Can we call by my house?" He was asking Lund, but it was Armstrong, behind the wheel, who answered.

"You won't need anything with you at this stage. We can always come back to the house."

165

"It's only a short . . ." But Conway saw the steady hands on the wheel and knew that the man was not open to persuasion. Lund gazed out of the window, ignoring him. So it was to be that way. Conway felt for his handkerchief; the carefully folded one in the little note pocket at the belt-line of his trousers. He had seen on television that suspects were made to empty their pockets before they were taken to the cells. He did not know whether that would happen before or after they questioned him. He didn't even know whether they would find the handkerchief at all but he saw no point in waiting to find out.

He lifted the cloth to his nose and wriggled the capsules out into his mouth. They were large medicinal capsules used at Net-tiscombe by the thousand but now each contained 500mg of potassium cyanide. Three of them held five times the lethal dose and he grimaced as he tried to bite and swallow at the same time. Lund turned sharply at the queer noise that he made but by then it was too late. Conway knew nothing of the probing fingers in his mouth or the futile race through the Cambridge streets. He was dead long before they got him to hospital.

THIRTEEN

"I CAN'T BE too hard on the Cambridge pair," Daintry was saying, an hour after Conway's suicide. "They were going by the book, I gather. They can't shove everybody in a strait jacket for starters. He was evidently prepared for it, was obviously our man."

"The question is," Randolph said rather sourly, "was he the only man?"

"I know how you feel, James. I was as keen to hear him talk as you were."

"Frits de Wet is going to be less than pleased with us again."

"He's a stroppy little bugger, that one, but he seems to have friends in high places."

"Not friends exactly. He sits on a sensitive spot, that's all."

"Well, I shall have to keep him in the picture. I've agreed to that."

"Of course. I've been leaned on myself. I promised him full involvement but I still think we should make the decisions first and involve him afterwards."

"Absolutely. So we're back to Tyler. Do we pull him in or do we let it run? I'm assuming your man has the tape by now — there's been nothing over the monitors about it."

"We got it to him this morning. He's been told not to waste any time."

"I'm glad to hear it. I can't keep the present team down there much longer; I'd have to downgrade it at least."

"Are you saying that you'd rather move in? It would please de Wet — especially when he learns about Conway."

"It's tempting. Just to pull him in again and grill him till he falls apart. We have more than enough on him now."

"True. But I don't need to remind you that our prisons are full of characters who never did talk."

"Perhaps we'll be lucky and there will be a revelation waiting for us at Conway's house. It's a village address. Old School House, a few miles out of Cambridge."

"Has it been . . ."

"Not yet. I've asked them to hold off. It's one of those things we must agree on right now. We can turn the place over or we can wait and see, but we can't wait too bloody long, James. We have to wrap things up soon."

Randolph looked troubled. "Let's take the worst scenario. Let's say you draw a blank at Conway's house and you take Tyler in again, but he won't or can't tell you anything that you don't already know. Will you be satisfied? Will you be sure that the case is closed? That there isn't a cache of that horror in somebody else's cupboard?"

Daintry waved the thought away. "You know I won't. That's why I went along with this caper in the first place. If your man can get Tyler to open everything up the easy way I'll be delighted, but we haven't had much yet, have we?"

"Except for exhibit A. I doubt we would have got a sample of his wares by threats and interrogation," Randolph said pointedly.

"I meant since then."

"Since then, very little, I must admit. But we've been withholding the stick and failing to provide the carrot. Half a million is an awfully expensive show to put on."

"It's an expensive show without that. It bothers me, that and the fact that it's going to break apart all by itself. I've got Cambridge-shire involved now as well as the South Africans levering about in high places. The press will be a whisker away when they hear we've had a suicide in a police car."

Randolph's blue eyes offered no insight to his thoughts and when at length he spoke it was half to himself. "A pity to waste the chance," he murmured, "at this stage."

"No question of anything being wasted," Daintry said firmly. "I just want the position to be fully understood. We need a deadline and it can't be too far off. If your tape trick doesn't work I think we should pull Tyler in and then I can get my crew on to other things."

Randolph blinked. "I'm sure twenty-four hours will be more than enough."

Daintry seemed relieved. "Twenty-four hours, then."

"Thank you."

Daintry nodded, satisfied.

"It would probably help if your Cambridge people could leave the house looking right. It shouldn't take many minutes."

They quickly agreed on what should be done and Daintry made to leave.

"Oh, and Ted."

"Now what?"

"Will you brief de Wet or shall I?"

Daintry smiled ruefully. "You have the advantage there; he doesn't know where to find you. He's probably waiting for me. Don't worry, I'll look after him."

Exactly thirty minutes later, in the south suburbs, Keith Tyler reached a decision of his own. Conversation had all but ceased during the past two days. The waiting game had become a contest: no more money — no deal. No deal — no more money and no more help. Impatience had given way to frustration and frustration had come to a head. Tyler was prepared to wait no longer.

The phone box was outside the post office.

"Smith." He spoke into the mouthpiece as if the name were a statement, an explanation.

For a moment there was silence and then Tamala's voice began to gabble. "Smith! Where the hell are you? Where have you been? We had given you up. Are you in trouble or what? No, wait, better we meet up. We have to get together again . . ."

Tyler listened, trying to make sense of the reaction, certain only that his own security must at all costs be protected. "I'm okay. No problem." He tried to speak lightly. "I can't say where I am but I'm back in business. Now, how is it with you? Can you still operate?"

It was Tamala's turn to be baffled. "Me? We've been waiting for you, man. I thought we had an arrangement. What went wrong? Listen, we can't talk like this. We have to meet up again . . ."

Tyler was dumbfounded. There was so much to be asked, so much to be told but he was stifled by the imperative to guard his secrets, to give nothing away. "Peter," he blurted. "Do you know a man called Peter?"

"Peter? Peter who? What is he to us? Are you with somebody now? Is he the one who was looking for you? No, I don't know. It doesn't matter. Listen, we *must* meet again. . . . Are you there? Hello?"

"Did you have trouble with the police? Did they try to keep you?" Tyler's voice became husky.

"Police? I don't know what you are talking about. I don't understand you. Listen: where we met last time — be there at eight o'clock. Can you get there? Can you do that? Hello? . . . Are you there?"

But Tyler put down the phone and pushed his ungainly frame on to the pavement. He scarcely noticed the woman who was waiting and he was not conscious of the expression on his face which caused her to back away from him.

While Gabriel Tamala was panting his news to Comrade Ulyanov, Keith Tyler walked the suburban streets more recklessly than he had done since his release from Albany Street. He made a pathetically easy subject for four Special Branch surveillance experts who found it hard to imagine how the gangling amateur could rate so highly on the priorities list.

Nothing short of a uniform or a police siren would have shaken Tyler during the twenty minutes that he circuited the blocks. His brain was fogged by confusion and mistrust. Reasoned thought, for a time, was beyond him. Had Tamala been play-acting or was his reaction genuine? Had he really known nothing of the arrest? Had he not even been questioned? He had sounded totally convincing and for a time Tyler was tempted to call him back and confirm a meeting: to bolt with the money he had and begin again with Tamala and his backers. But even as the notion entered his head he was despairing of his chances for they were the chances of a fugitive with no papers and no refuge. With the man called Peter, at least he seemed to be safe for the time being. But who was Peter? Did it matter? He was obviously not working in collaboration with Tamala and yet he had known all about the meeting in the tube and the agreement to supply another sample. That could only be explained if Peter's group had connections with the FAM or their backers. It confirmed what Tyler had suspected all along: somebody was trying to cut Tamala out of the deal. It also explained, to Tyler's satisfaction, why he had been discouraged from contacting the FAM. Well, if somebody else wanted the thing they were welcome to it, but why were the stupid bastards taking so long about it? And so his thoughts, like his footsteps, brought him back to start.

But if Tyler found no answer to his questions he at least reached a decision on what to do next. When two groups wanted what you had to offer you made the most of it: you played one against the other. As Tyler saw it his best course was to take Tamala at face value and use him to force the other's hand. The truth had still not crossed his mind. Not for an instant did the thought arise that the man called Peter could represent any sort of British authority.

Lawson sensed the change in Tyler as soon as he came in. There was a new and different energy beneath the sullen hostility. He came over to face him — challenging.

"You've got a bloody nerve."

Lawson waited.

"Gabriel Tamala wasn't picked up. He hasn't been scared off either. He still wants to do business."

"Who's been telling you that?"

"He has. I called him."

"You didn't tell him where you are . . "

"Of course not. I'm not stupid."

Lawson shrugged. "All right," he said, as if it were not worth arguing about. "What are you going to do about it?"

"That depends on you. I've given your mob long enough. If they haven't got the ready I'll go back to the FAM. So would you in my position."

Lawson got to his feet in a single, slow movement. He shook his head pityingly, derisively. "You poor bloody fool. I'd never have got myself into your position."

It was the tone and Lawson's total composure rather than the words which had most effect on Tyler. For the second time that day he felt the prickling unease that was the prelude to alarm. With awful certainty he knew that he was about to hear something that would shake him still further.

"I'm not interested in what you might have done," he retorted bravely. "It's what you should be doing that interests me. Whoever you represent is going to lose out, I'm warning you, I've waited long enough."

Lawson regarded him dispassionately. "How many of you are involved in this?" It was a question he had asked before — directly and otherwise.

"I've told you, that's something you'll never know."

Lawson's expression hardened. "I know what you told me but things have changed. You see, if the people I represent have lost out, it's because they backed a mug. They put me on to you. You are a loser, Tyler. You are the biggest bloody loser I ever met."

The alarm was now total. Tyler felt his gut tighten. "What are you trying to say?"

Lawson turned away, satisfied that he had the other thoroughly softened up. "Let me try it this way," he said carefully. "How many people could cut you out of this deal? How many would be better off with you out of the way? Worse still, how many do you depend on?"

"What are you getting at? If you have something to say — say it. I'm not in the mood for guessing games."

"I'm asking you a question, Tyler. It matters. Believe me, this is no game."

But Tyler was still not to be drawn. His response to interrogation was virtually automatic: his defence became stronger — *guard your secrets, give nothing away*. "I've said all I'm saying. If anything's changed it's up to you. Spell it out." But even as he spoke he dreaded what he might hear.

"A pity," Lawson said with distinct lack of sympathy. "I hoped you might tell me something encouraging. I hoped you might tell me you were the principal in your little enterprise. I hoped you might tell me that you were dependent on nobody, and especially not on your friend, Ralph Conway."

The effect on Keith Tyler was shattering. His jaw sagged and his eyes widened as if he had been hit. Then his lips began to move but so many questions were flashing through his brain that none was given voice.

Lawson turned away with a display of calculated disdain. "I'll make it easy for you," he said and he went over to the radio-cassette unit and switched on.

Conway's voice was unmistakable. *"The business matter that we discussed, Mr Tamala."*

"Yes."

"I'm calling to say that I accept your terms but we must have a different arrangement for the transfer; it's too risky."

"All right. We don't want to cause unnecessary trouble. Where do we make contact?" The voice was even more unmistakably that of Gabriel Tamala.

"I will call you back. Just be ready."

It did occur to Tyler, in the mental fusillade which followed, that the record might be fake but the idea seemed irrelevant. If they knew Ralph Conway well enough to fake his voice there would be no need for recordings at all; Conway would be putty in anybody's hands. That was the biggest bombshell of all — the fact that that timorous little egghead had found the nerve for a double-cross. *He must have believed I was dead*, Tyler told himself. *But maybe. . . . And then again it could be. . . . Or perhaps. . . .* But it was unfathomable.

Lawson allowed a minute or so for the full impact to be absorbed and then he quietly repeated the gibe: "Like I said, we seem to have backed a mug."

It still took Tyler a little time to find words. "I can check it out," he said eventually. "Even if he has done a deal he can't expect to get away with it. He must know what I'll do."

"That's between you and him," Lawson said steadily. "But if you've been dumped on your arse you've got a problem with me. Fifty thousand pounds' worth for a start."

Tyler was well aware of it, but giving up the money was not an option he was prepared to consider. When you had killed once you had nothing to lose. "When was all this?" He waved a hand at the sideboard where the unit was still hissing quietly through the rest of the tape. "How did you get it?"

Lawson threw back his head and laughed. "Jesus Christ. You're paranoid about your little secrets and you ask me a question like that! My group wanted an exclusive on this thing so naturally they kept an eye on the opposition — or an ear in this case."

"But when? How long . . ."

"Couple of days, we can't be sure. It's being worked on."

Tyler shook his head as if it would help to clear his brain. "But if the FAM have already got what they want why should they still be so keen to get back to me?'"

Lawson jabbed a finger. "That my friend, is exactly what concerns us. If you are out of it then their only motive is get you off your friend's back. It was probably part of his deal that they protect him by giving you a bad accident."

It seemed all too possible.

"On the other hand," Lawson continued, "if you can still deliver the stuff then they have a double motive for wanting you toes upwards. They want an exclusive as well."

That was also disturbingly plausible.

"All I want to know," Lawson went on, "is whether you still have anything to offer. If not I'll take the fifty grand and wish you luck but if you can still deliver you'd better prove it fast, bloody fast."

"And what about . . ."

Lawson bounced his palm off his forehead in exasperation. "You're impossible! You're between the biggest bloody rock and the hardest place imaginable and you still try to call the shots. For Christ's sake use your head. I'm giving you a chance. Whatever you've got can't be worth what it was before you all started peddling the stuff. We found out about Conway. How many more? You have lost control — if you ever had it. You're into a salvage operation now."

And Tyler could not deny any of it. What he felt at that moment, besides a sickening sense of betrayal, was something close to panic as he searched frantically for a new direction. "It's a hitch; nothing more than that. I can straighten it out, you'll see." He tried to sound confident.

"Well, I'm glad you think so," Lawson said with heavy sarcasm. "And what do you intend to do? Ring up and say please explain what you are up to?"

Tyler hesitated but could think of no other way. "I'll go there," he said decisively. "I'll find out for myself." And then he added, "Oh, I know you'll be coming. I can't stop you following me so you might as well provide the transport."

"Well at least that makes some sense," Lawson agreed. "And where are we going?"

"You'll see soon enough."

"I want to know the risk before I go anywhere," Lawson said flatly.

"There is no risk, unless we get stopped by the police. We have to go through town but we can leave after dark."

Lawson considered. "Everything is a risk now. Tell me this much: if Conway hasn't already delivered, how many others can screw you up?"

"Nobody," Tyler said emphatically. Under the circumstances it seemed a safe thing to say.

Nobody. Framed in his headphones the eavesdropper's smile was one of pure delight. "And about bloody time," he breathed. Within five minutes Daintry himself had heard the vital words and was patching them through on a direct line to James Randolph.

Randolph listened and approved.

Daintry enthused with him. "He did a good job, your man. Full marks. We might as well let him run the whole course. I'm sure you agree."

Randolph scarcely paused. "Certainly. I want to see where he goes, Ted. We still don't know that it's Conway's house. They may well have another depot."

"Right. I'll get organized. We'll tail them, of course, and stake out the house."

"Keep in touch." There were times when Randolph was less than content to remain in the wings.

Neither man believed there was any great risk of losing Tyler at that stage. The car he would travel in was still transmitting a strong signal, very experienced men would be in the tailing cars, and the stake-out of Conway's house would be thorough. Moreover, both Randolph and Daintry were now content to depend on Peter Lawson.

They started the journey just before lighting-up time. Two tailing cars moved after them as soon as they turned out of the cul-de-sac on to the main road. Lawson was driving. Tyler was in the front passenger seat and the fifty thousand pounds was, by agreement, in the locked boot; neither man was going to bolt at a traffic stop — at least not with the cash.

Tyler gave directions section by section but it soon became apparent that they were heading for the M25 and the fastest route to Cambridge.

Traffic was heavy and again Lawson was impressed by the skill of the Special Branch drivers. Somewhere in the headlights strung out behind were those of two police cars and before they reached Cambridge Lawson had learned to pick them out. They were never far away but never very close.

Beyond Cambridge, Tyler became preoccupied by powerful recollections of that earlier journey. He saw the road ahead through a swirling white mist that did not exist. He felt its chill in the warm of the car. He saw the small, dark shape of a dead hare and heard again the voice of Ralph Conway, *when you hit a smooth patch you can end up in the ditch* . . . Conway!

"We turn right here." Tyler broke the silence and jolted himself back to the present. They were travelling much faster than they had done on that earlier night. It was well over a year ago now. It seemed much more. They passed the pub on the right sooner than Tyler expected and he told Lawson to slow down. "I don't want to miss the turn."

His mouth had gone dry and he moistened his lips. It was not fear, he assured himself. He was tense but not afraid. What he had done once, with a hammer, he could do again if he had to. The tension would help him. He would not be scared. To some extent it was true.

Lawson could see no following lights and he wondered if the tails could be driving on side-lights. He hoped the turn would not be so sudden that they would lose him. He decided to take it slowly and keep his lights on full beam.

"Dip your lights," Tyler said. "I think the turn is somewhere here. Dip your lights."

"What the hell for?"

"Just dip the bloody things. We're nearly there. I want to stop short without lighting up half the district."

Lawson pressed the switch just as he swung into the turn. Then he flashed the beam again briefly, as if he'd needed it.

"Slow right down. There's a place you can pull off soon — there — now. Get right in, behind those trees. We'll walk the last bit." Tyler carried a small torch but they had no need of it then: the edge of the road was plain enough and after a few minutes the lights of Ketley were in view.

"Cut through here," Tyler said softly and they stepped across the verge to approach Conway's house from the side. The house was in darkness. Tyler led the way round the back and began to examine the windows. From somewhere across the green they could hear commercials on somebody's television. "Seems to be locked" Tyler muttered. "But they're easy to open. Have you got a knife?"

Lawson hesitated and then handed him a pocket knife, holding the torch himself with a hand cupped over the end to cut down the light. Tyler slipped the blade between the old sash window frames and pushed the catch aside. He jerked at the lower frame until it suddenly slid upwards. The noise was appalling. They stood stock still, listening. The television had gone quieter. Lawson crept round to the front and peered across the green. Nothing was moving.

"It's all right," he told Tyler. "All clear."

"No dog," Tyler said.

"What?"

"He has a dog. It can't be here."

"Lucky then."

Tyler was still standing by the open window. One of them had to go first. A few hundred yards away the car was parked with fifty thousand pounds in the boot. Lawson had the key.

"You go first," Tyler said.

Lawson smiled to himself, placed a hand on Tyler's shoulder and heaved himself smoothly on to the sill. He swung his legs over and helped Tyler to follow. "Where to?" he said softly.

"Upstairs, there's a sort of laboratory." Tyler took the torch and led the way. The door at the top of the stairs was open and in the roving beam they surveyed the assorted glassware and oddments of apparatus that were arranged on shelves and on a large, central table. It was unimpressive; nothing more, to Lawson's eye, than a makeshift school chemistry lab. Tyler opened two cupboards and

177

checked the covered storage area beneath the sink. There was no sign of recent use. Cleaning cloths were dry and hard. In fact, Conway had done nothing in his private laboratory for months.

"He wouldn't leave the stuff lying about, would he?"

"Just looking round. It will be in an old safe — there look."

In the dim yellow light Lawson looked at the archaic Chubb. A cracksman's joy and, for Peter Lawson, a supreme irony. On the other side of the law he had never found anything so easy. "And how are we supposed to get into that?" he asked innocently.

Tyler said nothing. If Conway had really gone, the cultures had probably gone too. He was preparing himself for the worst. It might be worth taking the safe. Perhaps they could get it down the stairs on a mattress and manoeuvre it into the car with an improvised ramp, but if Conway had gone there seemed little chance of finding the cultures inside. He fingered the door. It moved a fraction. He pulled it open and found the safe empty. From the darkness behind he heard Lawson's sibilant snort of disgust. "He's gone and taken the stuff with him."

Tyler turned and said the first thing he could think of. "We're not beaten yet. He only kept small samples in the safe. The bulk store is underground." He hoped it sounded convincing. He had no idea that there was actually some truth in it. He was not really thinking any more, only preparing himself for what he had to do. It had been different last time, not deliberate, not cold blooded. Well this time it would be intentional and it would have to be done quietly. He felt his heart thudding again. That would go away. It was like stage fright; it came before the thing but went away when you actually did it. "Go ahead," he said, and shone the torch towards the door.

Lawson stepped forward, seeing his own hulking shadow above the stairs. Tyler had already noticed the pestle and mortar. It was big and heavy, like a relic from ancient alchemy. A curio, probably. He picked up the pestle and slipped it, like a truncheon, into his trousers pocket. At the foot of the stairs Lawson waited for the light, watching Tyler come down. "Where to now?" he whispered.

"Out again. No, wait." Tyler went through to the lounge and kitchen, torchlight and shadows dancing on the walls ahead of him. In the kitchen he opened the fridge door. It was empty and no light came on. Had he needed confirmation that Conway had really gone, that was it. He felt the pestle and flashed the torch around the kitchen. There was no better weapon in sight. Without cash and unable to reveal his identity, Tyler knew he would be lost; no better off than the desperate souls who were hunted down on the moors after a few days of miserable freedom. Fifty thousand pounds was a lot better than nothing. It could buy time and, through Tamala, he might locate Conway and outwit them both. If he could stay free he would survive, and they could not ignore him because he knew too much. But to survive he needed cash. Lawson was now standing at the kitchen door.

"Okay," Tyler said. "Outside again."

Lawson stood back, letting him light the way. At the window he said, "You'll want to go first this time."

Tyler nodded and climbed through. He had already decided where to do it. And how it should be done. Peter was a heavy man to move. Let him get there on his feet. It could be weeks before they found his body, and who could connect the killing with Keith Tyler?

Lawson came effortlessly through the window. "Now what?"

"Along here." Tyler picked his way along the side of the building showing scarcely any light at all between his fingers. "There, see?" On the ground the rusted, corrugated sheets had grass growing over the edges. "There's a cellar underneath."

Tyler pulled at the top sheet and it made a loud scraping noise. They both froze. It was completely quiet now except for a dog barking, far off.

"Take the other end. Lift them, don't let them scrape." Together they removed the sheets and stacked them gently to one side. The wooden trapdoor looked strong and solid. The padlock was gleaming like a new one. Tyler shone a thin beam over it then quickly changed the torch to his left hand, pressing it against his hip to hide the tremor. "What do you think? Can we open it?" His voice was thick and strange. "Well, what do you think?"

Lawson stared down at the lock and the heavy bolt which held the trapdoor and then he slowly crouched to examine it, positioning himself at Tyler's side.

The blow never connected. Lawson was waiting. He saw Tyler shift his balance, was ready for the movement of the torch beam that would signal the attack. He came up hard and fast, using all the power of his legs and back and grabbing for the right wrist as he had been trained to do. It was a classic technique for disarming an assailant but Tyler was strong and not easily handled. He dropped the torch and began to gouge and punch with his left hand. Lawson hit him once, very hard. Tyler slumped and the pestle clattered down on the sheets of iron.

Lights came on then and someone called out. Two figures came from the blackness of the garden and bent over Tyler, holding his arms and searching his pockets. Somebody clapped a hand on Lawson's shoulder and said "good man". There were running footsteps, voices and torchlights on all sides. One man knelt at the trapdoor just as another took Lawson's sleeve and a low voice said, "I think you can make a quiet exit now." Lawson recognized the assured tones of Neville Brigham, a veteran in Randolph's team of fieldmen. He stretched out a welcoming hand and together they withdrew towards the rear of the house.

FOURTEEN

IT TOOK THE Special Branch man no time at all to remove the padlock. He drew back the thick bolt and yanked at the iron ring on the trapdoor. From his position he could not see the chain that was suspended on a snap-link under the wood. Had he seen it he would have found that it was easily disengaged by slipping a hand under the slightly raised door. The other end of the chain was attached to a steel rod which pivoted on top of a large crate. He knew nothing of that either. If he had known he would have been very careful indeed. But in his ignorance he just lifted the door. He lifted until the steel rod moved on its fulcrum and his world was filled with blinding light and shattering noise and he knew no more at all.

It is doubtful whether anybody at that time knew what had happened and it is unlikely that anyone could have reached any conclusions during the moments of shock and subsequent clamour. It seems probable that Keith Tyler just found himself lying in the grass with his two escorts some yards away in a similar position. But he was not slow in coming to his senses. Tyler was one of the first on his feet and was running for tree cover before the policemen realized they no longer had him.

Lawson and Brigham had their backs to the cellar when the explosion occurred. They felt relatively little of it but, like everyone else, they flung themselves down instinctively when the blast filled the air with light and flying debris. The trapdoor was blown to pieces. The cellar floor had a small, shallow bomb crater but the walls remained intact. The force of the explosion was directed upwards as was the geyser of flame which followed. There was little surrounding damage except for smashed windows and a leg injury caused by a splinter of wood.

Tyler ran impulsively, jinking and leaping for the deepest shadows. He had no clear intentions beyond escape. Shock and confusion had even robbed him of the resolve that was his mainstay. Keith Tyler was, quite literally, running scared.

Lawson was on his feet but could see nothing beyond the belching flames. Half circling the fire he found one man leaning on a tree holding his thigh, unable to walk. Two others he could see in silhouette trying to shield themselves against the heat while they pulled clear the limp body of a colleague. Another was running towards the shadows at the end of the overgrown garden. Lawson went after him.

Facing the darkness Tyler slowed and tried to run at a crouch so that he could see the position of the trees against the sky. He failed to see, directly in front of him, the still figure of a man who all along had been keeping a distant view of proceedings. *Keep a low profile, they had said. Come along by all means but keep out of the action. You'll get your chance when the operation is over*, they had told him.

Frits de Wet now stepped forward. He had been well clear of the blast; startled by it but otherwise unaffected. He had been watching the torchlit figure of Keith Tyler being led away when the bomb went off. After the flash, the fire had provided a backlit view of a stage on which Tyler had become the principal actor. He had watched him lurch to his feet and begin his desperate run for the darkness and for the waiting arms of the Afrikaner.

If Tyler had not already been hurt, dazed and thoroughly demoralized de Wet would not have found him so easy to deal with. As it was he tripped him and after a few seconds' fumbling in the dark he managed to pin him down with an unbreakable hold on his arm and neck.

Tyler did not catch the words that de Wet hissed in his ear but he thought the word 'stuff' was one of them. It flashed through his fuddled brain that perhaps this was not the police but one of Peter's men. "Let me go. Conway . . . taken it . . . let me go." He was choking.

De Wet relaxed his grip a fraction, realizing that Tyler had no idea who was holding him. "Who else had it?"

"Conway . . . only Conway. I'll find him for . . . let me go . . . please."

"Can you make the stuff?"

"No. Yes . . . I might. I'll try. But let me go. I can . . . find out."

De Wet shifted his grip. "Yes," he whispered. "Yes, one day you might just manage to do that." And calmly and deliberately he broke Tyler's neck.

Lawson and a Special Branch man arrived together. The policeman had a torch. At once they examined Tyler's body, seeing the angle of the head, feeling for a pulse.

"He's dead," de Wet told them.

"You've killed him."

"It must have been the bomb. Something hit him," he said with no pretence at conviction.

"You broke his bloody neck!"

"Who is this?" Lawson asked, for he had never before seen or heard of de Wet.

But before the policeman could answer another figure appeared. "Leave it," he said to Lawson. "He's an accredited diplomat. Let's make that quiet exit."

Lawson was about to protest but Brigham took him by the sleeve. "Leave it," he said firmly. "Let's go."

The blaze had spread to the house before the fire engines arrived. From a forensic point of view it was unfortunate because the fire in the cellar died down rather abruptly after the last butane cylinder burst. But the hosing of the house filled the cellar with water and delayed the scientists' work. Among the soaking debris they found charred fragments of human bone, but the body of Barry Chandler was never positively identified. There was ample evidence of glassware but it was impossible to say whether the old wine bottles had contained anything interesting. The most important items were several lengths of steel pipe found in association with broken glass phials. Neither the journalists nor the excited residents of Ketley ever got to know about those specimens. The site was cordoned off and uniformed police kept sightseers well away.

The official version, which was reported nationwide, was expanded, illustrated and given sensation status in the local papers; photographs of the fire-damaged house were easy to obtain. The drama failed to surprise some of the Ketley people, or so they claimed. They had always suspected Conway was up to no good, all by himself in that old school house. They had always said he was not normal, that one. There were rumours that he might have smuggled dangerous germs out of the Nettiscombe works, but nothing was ever reported missing and no sort of warnings were issued. The bomb had been real enough, though. A pity, they all agreed, that the two of them hadn't blown themselves up earlier with their home-made bombs and then that policeman wouldn't have been killed. Bloody terrorists.

Frits de Wet, on his hurried departure for Pretoria, carried the main newspapers with him, but he was preoccupied with uncertainties about his own future so he gave them less than his full attention. Two insignificant but not unrelated events would have interested him even less. In the village of Trumpington, near Cambridge, a Miss Samantha Crowther received a present from the RSPCA in recognition of the good home she could provide for it. It was a black and white mongrel dog.

And in Karaganda, one Rina Bykov, who had lived with her brother's family for four years, was formally notified that her husband had died in hospital after being involved in a prison brawl. She was instructed to collect a parcel from the railway station and guessed what it would be. She was not therefore disappointed to find a worthless bundle of her late husband's belongings.

By that time Frits de Wet had been promoted.